The odds were two against one—but Jess evened them out fast. One of the bushwackers took off after Jess's first shot, fleeing hell-for-leather on his mount.

The other was lying gut-shot in the dust. All he could do was ask Jess to put him out of his misery. And when Jess wouldn't, the dying man begged, "Gimme my gun. Let me do it. I'll put it to my own head. For God's sake, Mister."

Jess looked at the man on the blood-muddy ground for a sick moment, then found the gun. He placed it in the man's right hand and turned away.

"Damn you!" shrieked the fallen gunman. "I'll take you with me to hell!"

As the bullet slammed into him, Jess McClaren realized *you could trust no one—unless he was dead. . . .*

THE
BLOODY
SANDS
E. Z. Woods
A SIGNET BOOK
NEW AMERICAN LIBRARY

PUBLISHER'S NOTE

This book is a work of fiction. Names, characters, places, and incidents either are the product of the author's imagination or are used fictitiously, and any resemblance to actual persons, living or dead, events, or locales is entirely coincidental.

NAL BOOKS ARE AVAILABLE AT QUANTITY DISCOUNTS WHEN USED TO PROMOTE PRODUCTS OR SERVICES. FOR INFORMATION PLEASE WRITE TO PREMIUM MARKETING DIVISION, NEW AMERICAN LIBRARY, 1633 BROADWAY, NEW YORK, NEW YORK 10019.

SIGNET TRADEMARK REG. U.S. PAT. OFF. AND FOREIGN COUNTRIES
REGISTERED TRADEMARK—MARCA REGISTRADA
HECHO EN CHICAGO, U.S.A.

SIGNET, SIGNET CLASSIC, MENTOR, ONYX, PLUME, MERIDIAN and NAL BOOKS are published by NAL PENGUIN INC., 1633 Broadway, New York, New York 10019

First Printing, April, 1988

1 2 3 4 5 6 7 8 9

PRINTED IN THE UNITED STATES OF AMERICA

Chapter One

As the last red and gold light was snuffed out of the sky to the west, a breeze sprang up, sighing across the pine- and spruce-forested ridge. Smells rose from the little settlement in the canyon below; smoke from supper fires within cabins scattered upon the slopes and in meadows along the stream, dust stirring in corrals where bony-spined cows bawled to be fed and milked, the dry, resinous scent of mountain growth, brittle for want of rain. Although the day was gone, the August heat gave way slowly.

The tall man waiting on the ridge caught the tangy odor of frying pork. Hunger tightened his belly. His last cold, hurried meal had been before dawn, and today's ride had been long and fast. Yet for the last hour he had halted in this shadowed clump of oak without making a fire even for coffee. Waiting with iron patience near his horses, he watched his back trail, alert for riders entering the mountain village.

At full dark the man unfolded his lean body and stood. Still dissatisfied, although he had seen nothing at all out of the ordinary, he moved to the big bay stallion grazing nearby on the sparse dry grass. He jerked tight the loosened cinch, slipped the curb bit into the animal's mouth and the bridle over the black-tipped, alert ears. He paused for an instant with all senses strained, not so much listening as feeling about him for the source of his uneasiness. But there was nothing, only the sudden clatter of a grasshopper landing in dry careless weed. The tall man swung lightly into his saddle.

There was a lead rope wrapped around the horn. He took up the slack and brought a young mare up alongside. The rangy bay stepped forward eagerly. The rider allowed his horse to pick its surefooted way down the steep, wooded slope, and onto the narrow wagon road. Both horses eased into a fox-trot toward a dwelling that was set back from the road.

Lantern light fell from the narrow front windows of the log house with its steeply pitched, shingled roof. There was a lean-to at one side. A small window, uncurtained and in need of washing, surveyed the road.

As the rider turned his horse toward the house, the light went out. Someone called, "State your business, stranger!"

A rifle barrel showed itself through a missing pane, and instinctively the horseman reached for his saddlegun.

"Now, don't touch that, son, unless you mean to use it," cautioned the voice, almost kindly. "I got you square in my sights, an' I don't miss much."

Deftly the horseman controlled the bay's dancing steps, lifting both hands and reins high enough to be visible to the watcher. "I want no trouble, mister," he said. "A man is to meet me at Toland's place."

There was a short silence. "I'm Toland. Who is it said he'd meet you here?"

"Man name of Quilter. Rides for Mr. Joe Ed Whitley."

"Uh-huh. An' who might you be?"

"McClaren. Jess McClaren."

Another silence, the watcher apparently studying his visitor, from the dusty Stetson, past the thin face with its narrow gray eyes and light brown beard and mustache, to the wide-shouldered body. At last the rifle barrel was withdrawn. McClaren waited until the front door creaked open. A bald, elderly man beckoned to him.

Jess reined the stallion to the hitch rail and dismounted.

The older man, still grasping his gun, glanced about in the darkness. "I'll take the horses around to the barn. Go in. No sir! Jest leave it," he instructed sharply as Jess started to remove the .30-.30 Winchester from his saddle.

The older man led both horses at a trot toward a small barn and corral back of the cabin.

Jess eased his Colt out of the holster and stepped inside the dark house, kicking the door shut behind him. Someone moved in the room. McClaren stood still, fixing the location of the sounds.

A match flared. Jess saw a large, gray-haired woman bent over an oil lamp. She glanced at Jess, her face impassive. Touching the match to the wick, she replaced the lamp chimney. Feeling foolish, Jess reholstered his gun.

The door creaked. Toland came in carrying Jess's rifle, and his own Henry. He carefully placed the Winchester out of Jess's reach.

The old man was dressed in faded red long johns and patched trousers, galluses hooked over bent shoulders. An old Peacemaker was stuck in his waistband. Apparently folks hereabouts did not rest easy in their beds of a night.

"You'd best lay down again, Mr. Toland," the woman murmured.

Toland barred the door. "Go bring us coffee, Ma." He looked at Jess. "I been down with my head under me with the summer complaint, but I'm okay now."

Jess doubted it. Toland's face was drawn, his eyes feverish.

"Where can I find Quilter?" Jess asked.

Toland shrugged and evaded the question. "Say now, them are right fine horses you got. I give 'em a little prairie hay."

"Thanks."

"Come sit to the table, son."

Toland led the way into the next room. This apparently was used for both sleeping and eating. There was a round oak table in the center of the square, high-ceilinged room whose walls had been pasted over with newspaper in an effort to keep out winter drafts. In the corner stood a tarnished brass bed, the quilts somewhat disarranged. McClaren guessed that Toland had been resting there when he arrived. There was a big wood heater to one side. The winters must be miserable in this high valley.

Jess removed his hat and sat at the table. Gratefully he accepted the coffee Mrs. Toland brought from the kitchen and handed him.

"Ma, see can you scare us up something to eat. We got any of that venison left? I feel like I might could eat something tonight."

She nodded and turned away. Toland confided to Jess, "It's been three, four days since anythin' I et stayed down. I been as weak as a day-old dogie."

"No call for you to leave a sickbed to meet me," Jess said. Then, dryly, "You folks are almighty cautious hereabouts."

Toland worked his toothless gums from side to side and rubbed at a gray stubble of beard. "Well sir, in Lincoln County a man cain't afford to lie abed when there's ary stranger about. Ain't more'n a few years ago the Tunstall and Murphy feud was finished. It was only in eighty-one that Pat Garrett laid Billy Bonney in his grave, an' there's some as says he never done it at all, that Billy's still alive, down in Mexico, maybe." Toland pursed his lips thoughtfully.

"They's many a man in these hills who got crossways with 'at young killer back then, and wouldn't like to see him show up again. Then there's the big ranchers and them town politicians down to Las Cruces. They're trying, some swears, to shove out the small ranchers, accusing them of rustling and sech like. But them small operators is mostly Texans, an' I guess I don't have to tell you the stamp of men they are. They don't push easy. It's uneasy times. Yessir, uneasy times."

Toland gave Jess a quick look, his eyes squirrel bright under the straggly gray brows. "You headed over the mountains to Joe Ed's place?"

Jess dodged the query with one of his own. "Have you talked to Mr. Whitley? I had his letter some weeks back, and he said his man Quilter would be waiting for me here along about now. I don't care to do a whole lot o' waiting."

Toland sipped noisily at his coffee, then shot a swift, shrewd glance at his guest. "Ain't much use you awaiting on Quilter. He ain't ever going no place again. He was bushwhacked ten days ago."

Jess half-rose, his long body tensing. "Why didn't you tell me that straight off, Toland? Who killed Quilter?"

The older man sighed regretfully and slid the old handgun over the edge of the table. "Set yourself down, Mr. McClaren. Jest you set down an' we'll talk, quiet like. I didn't mention what happened to Quilter because I don't tell everything I know to every drifter. It ain't smart. An' I don't know who got Quilter, though I have my notions. Could have been you fer that matter. Thought I'd jest watch you fer a spell. I pride myself I know what a man's eyes is saying even when his mouth says something else." Toothlessly, he grinned.

Mrs. Toland came into the room carrying plates of food, which she set in front of the men. Toland laid down his gun to grasp a fork. "I'm thinking you didn't know Quilter was in his grave, an' I'm willing to set here and give you some supper and enjoy a po-lite confab until Whitley sends fer you. If he ever does. I ain't had no word on it, though it could be Quilter was on his way here to set it up when them sneaking coyotes blasted him. If you are expected, Joe Ed will send somebody, likely."

With an effort, Jess controlled his aggravation. "Mr. Toland, the letter Joe Ed Whitley sent my pa will prove I was told to come here. It's in my shirt pocket—"

"Jest you set easy, son. Ma, you see if there's a letter there."

As calmly as if their conversation was about the drought or the price of cows, she obeyed her husband, standing behind Jess to fish quickly in his pocket. She handed the creased letter to Toland and without being asked got his eyeglasses from a shelf on which lay a worn family Bible.

Toland spread out the paper and began to puzzle out the writing. Jess dug into the supper, chewing the hot, tender meat and fried potatoes with pleasure. Mrs. Toland refilled his coffee cup, accepting his thanks without expression.

Jess thought about the letter, and the events that

brought him here, so far from the little horse ranch he'd called home in the cedar brakes west of Austin.

Addressed to Jess's pa, the letter had arrived the week after Morgan McClaren's funeral. The ranch was already sold. Not much use to keep it now. In his last months Jess's father had gambled away the best stock, including the bay thoroughbred stud known across half of Texas for his tough, fast colts.

No use even to blame Morgan for losing the horses. Gambling had been a craving with Pa, the way some men crave drink. But the loss of the stud had hurt. After Morgan's death Jess took what he could get for the land and bought the bay back. He paid too much for Capitan, but managed to also purchase one of the four-year-old mares Jess and Morgan had recently bought from a breeder of fine horses near Chihuahua, Mexico. Unaware that she was worth almost as much as the stallion, the owner let Jess have her at a bargain.

When the letter from Whitley arrived, Jess opened it. It was written in smudged pencil, the hand was large and uneven.

> *Morgan, my old friend,*
>
> *I hear you have a son is some good with a gun. I could sure use him here, if he could come. Tell him, from Roswell, Lincoln County, New Mexico territory, come west into the mountains to Bonita City, first week in August, John Toland's place, first cabin, west side of the road. Mac Quilter will meet him and bring him on. Don't tell no one his business is with me. Warn your boy, ride fast, watch good behind him.*
>
> *Thanks,*
> *Joe Ed Whitley*

Jess had recognized the name. Morgan had often spoken of Whitley. Both men had fought for the Confederacy. Whitley had once saved Morgan McClaren's life, carrying him off a bloody battlefield under cannon fire. Together they came to Texas after the defeat. Joe Ed soon moved on. Morgan, who'd married a Texas girl, stayed, built up the ranch, raised his son. When his wife died, he began to let things go, and his gambling eroded away any profit from the horses.

Jess frowned. How had Whitley learned of Jess's skill with a gun? It had to be word of the trouble with the Montwell brothers, shiftless ne'er-do-wells who hung out in the limestone hills. They'd tried to ambush Morgan after he won from them at poker. Jess was walking behind Morgan as they left the saloon. The Montwells, waiting in the street, opened up without warning, and slugs splintered the wooden door frame to right and left of Jess's pa. Jess jerked Morgan behind him and drew his gun in the same movement. The Colt bucked in his hand, and left both attackers dead in the mud of the town's main street. Morgan had taken a bullet through his shoulder, and Jess would have a scar along his left jaw, under the beard, for the rest of his life.

It was disturbing that the story of the shoot-out, something Jess would have given much to avoid, had traveled so far.

Yet all that was beside the point. As Morgan's son, Jess owed something to Joe Whitley. And he had no desire to stay in Austin. Maybe Lincoln County, New Mexico territory, was as good a place as any to go.

Jess had packed grub for the trip, tied a couple of changes of clothing in his bedroll. All the household goods had sold with the ranch. Jess gave everything else except Morgan's handgun and rifles, his mother's gold locket and Bible, to Morgan's best friend, Henry Garth. He sold the guns, placed the Bible and locket in a saddlebag, and was on his way.

He had ridden hard, careful only not to overtax his horses, to meet the time specified in Whitley's letter. It was sure as hell galling to get here and be thwarted by a nervous old man with a rusty six-shooter. He was ready to do whatever Joe Ed Whitley wanted of him, if it could be done in honor. But Jess was restless, eager to be done with obligations, to strike out and satisfy the longing he'd had to ignore these past few years, the longing to be on the move.

Toland finished with the letter, looked at Jess, eyes

crinkling with deep thought behind the wire-rimmed spectacles. Calmly he handed the letter to his wife. "Bertha, burn this," he said.

The woman took the paper and left the room. There was the sound of a stove lid being removed and then clanged back into place.

"Maybe you'll see fit to tell me what is your right to do that?" Jess's voice was dangerously quiet.

Toland shrugged. "That paper could git you in trouble. Might be someone has already seen it. You stay in one o' them ho-tels down there to Roswell?"

Puzzled, Jess nodded, then remembered that returning to his room after supper in a cantina, he'd felt uneasy, like someone had been in his room, though he found no sign. But the note had been there, in the pocket of the shirt he'd changed out of. Could someone, curious about a stranger in town, have done a bit of checking?

"And—supposing that's so?" he said.

"Wellsir," Toland said slowly, "it seems Joe Ed has a enemy or two. Maybe some he don't even suspect. And word travels fast in the territory. I myself knew a stranger was headed thisaway two days past. If that there note was to be read by the wrong person, word might jest be sent Joe Ed had help on the way. Might be you wouldn't ever reach J-bar-W."

Jess leaned back and watched his host. It surely was not possible that Toland knew about the two riders who had followed McClaren since leaving Roswell's dusty streets. Who those men were or what they were after, Jess had no notion. Nor were they anxious to come up and introduce themselves. They had paralleled his trail for two days, hanging back just out of reach of rifle fire. Jess thought he might have lost them when he entered the tangled canyons of the high country, this side of Lincoln's rounded, brush-studded hills. He had deliberately left the main trails and traveled cross-country, putting the horses over flinty ground that would scarcely take a trace an Apache could have detected. He'd doubled back twice, once riding through a trickle of stream along its sheer stone bed, though the water-slick footing made for slow going.

And today he had watched from the ridge above the village for any sign of the riders. They had not shown themselves, but Toland's remarks reawakened the gut-tightening sense of warning.

That gnawing tension made him doubly determined not to be held here indefinitely. If the mysterious riders were still scouting for him, it was certain they would know his horses. Toland had put them out of sight of the casual passerby. That was no guarantee a determined searcher couldn't find them.

As Jess was considering how to overpower Toland, without hurting the old man, there was a whistle from outside. Toland handed his gun to his wife. She held it steadily upon Jess, while Toland hitched up his galluses and went out.

He was back in moments with a short, red-faced man whose hair matched his complexion. The newcomer greeted Mrs. Toland courteously before turning to look at Jess.

"This here's Red Warner," Toland grunted. "He rides for Whitley. Red, this feller says he's the man Whitley's waiting for."

"That so?" Warner studied Jess intently with small blue eyes. "What do I call you?"

"I'm Jess McClaren."

"Can you prove that?"

Jess controlled irritation, shrugged. "I had a letter from Joe Ed Whitley. Toland burned it."

Toland nodded. "Yep. They was a letter."

"You think he's McClaren?" Warner demanded of the older man.

"I don't rightly know. I reckon he coulda took that there letter off somebody else."

Jess stood so abruptly that his chair fell over. "Now, I have had about as much of this as I intend to put up with!"

He towered over the other men, his right hand resting near his Colt in spite of Bertha Toland's gun still pointed stolidly at him.

Warner frowned, but asked Toland, "How's he mounted?"

"Big American stud, a bay branded M-diamond-W.

Leading a fine black mare. Real good stock. Don't know as I've seed any better."

"That's McClaren's brand. Joe Ed marked it out for me."

"Them horses could be stolen."

Warner scratched his head. "Reckon I got no choice but to take this drifter to Joe Ed. He'll know him, maybe."

Toland nodded. "I'll saddle his horse. You keep an eye on 'im."

"Nah, let me do it. You look like you're pinin' fer your coffin. You hadn't ought to be up." He clapped his hat on and went out the back, spurs ringing.

In silence now, Toland took his gun from Bertha and leveled it at Jess until Warner gave a whistle from in front of the cabin. The old man motioned Jess toward the front door.

Jess didn't move. "You'll put that gun down and hand me my rifle, Toland, or I'll stay right here until you drop over," he said with quiet menace.

Toland hesitated, then obeyed. As he handed Jess's Winchester to him, there was no fear, only amusement, in his eyes, though he must have known he had pushed his visitor to the end of patience. Jess grinned, then nodded to the big woman who watched him for the first time with some emotion showing in her heavy face. She was afraid, McClaren saw, afraid for her man. It showed in the way she twisted her apron and had her lips sucked in tight. It made him a little ashamed of his impatience.

"I thank you for the good meal, ma'am," he said gently. Taking his Stetson from the table, he turned and walked out of the small house into the chill of the mountain night.

Chapter Two

The narrow valley was still and dark. Stars glittered above the wooded ridges. Jess saw the bunched forms of horses in the lane in front of the house, the stallion looming tallest. The bay was sixteen hands high, with powerful quarters and chest, ample heart girth. His head was short for a thoroughbred, the space between intelligent eyes wide. Seen in daylight, Capitan was a blood bay, black below the knees, his mane and tail crow's wing dark.

The horse moved restively as if eager to travel. He nickered softly as Jess took the reins, and gave a quick, impatient leap forward as his rider's boot touched the stirrup. Lightly, Jess was in the saddle, reining the bay back in a half-circle spin that lifted both forefeet. He took the mare's lead rope from Warner's hand.

"Man, that there is some horse," breathed the cowboy. "If you stole him, I sure do not blame you."

"He'll carry a man to hell and back," Jess said. "Lead the way, Warner."

"I'll just come along behind," Warner said. "Follow the road up this here canyon until I tell you different."

Jess kneed the bay and struck out briskly. Dogs barked a challenge as they passed cabins. Jess felt watchers behind curtained windows, and knew that those watchers would not relax upon their meager beds until the sound of hoofbeats faded into silence.

They had left the last of the dwellings when Warner indicated a faint trail that led down to the wide, shallow, creek bed. They crossed the water, climbing out on rock so water-smoothed that the black mare Jess led had momentary trouble keeping her footing. They found a trail slanting up to the ridge, and for several miles they rode at a walk through the darkness of a tree-crowded trail.

In a small clearing, Warner spoke softly. "Pull up a minute." He moved his horse ahead of McClaren's, eyes seeming to search Jess's face as he brushed by. Was the man thinking that Jess might put a bullet in his back, as someone had put a bullet into a man called Quilter ten days past?

Warner led the way, swiftly now, down the slope to cross a wide, night-shrouded canyon and move into the dark mouth of another.

Jess could see little of his surroundings, and nothing of the path. Warner's dun pony was a ghostly shimmer ahead, seeming to vanish entirely at times as the trail bent back on itself or wound through saplings and brush. The night sky was alive with stars that seemed closer than was natural.

Steadily, with cat-footed sureness, the stud and the black mare trotted behind Warner's mount, mile after mile. The moonless night held the scent of evergreens and now and then the fresh, cold breath of the stream, mixed with a bitter odor of hoof-crushed weeds. Saddle leather creaked softly. Iron shoes rang against stone. Jess could see nothing plainly except the skyline, less dark than the steep canyon walls, which ended in a tangle of treetops.

Climbing into the head of the canyon, they rode out onto a wide, grassy ridge. Jess felt like a kid let out of a dark and lonely room, glad to be in the open again. Warner halted his horse, listening to the night sounds around them, unnecessarily raising a hand to caution Jess to stillness.

There was only the sigh of wind, the sleepy chirping of a bird somewhere in the thick boughs of an ancient juniper in whose shadow they had halted, a quick, light jingle of a curb chain as Capitan lowered his nose and rubbed it against his foreleg.

Nevertheless, Warner paused longer than was needed to give the horses a rest after the climb out of the canyon. Finally he moved his dun out.

Warner now spurred his mount to a gallop, risky in the dark. But the cowpony must have been over this trail many times. He moved at an easy, confident lope even over the worst of the trail that curved along the miles of crest from which enormous canyons fell away to the east and west. Capitan's long legs easily kept up. The mare cantered with light grace at Capitan's shoulder, the warm barrel of her body brushing McClaren's knee from time to time.

They traveled some five miles on the open ridgetop before Warner again called a halt. Once more the cowpuncher listened for whatever he expected to hear, and Jess strained his senses too. Was that the faint impact of a hoof on rock, somewhere behind them?

Capitan threw up his head, staring back along the crest. Quickly Warner put a gloved hand over the bay's flared nostrils, then urgently spurred away to one side. He seemed to have dropped off the face of the mountain. Capitan followed the dun downslope into a trail almost overgrown with piñon and juniper and buck brush. It would have been difficult to spot even in daylight. At night it was the next thing to invisible.

Leading sharply down into a canyon, the trail turned back like a woman's hairpin, thrust through thick brush that caught at the rider's clothing and stirrups. The horses were forced to push their way through tightly woven limbs. Jess worried about the noise the dry growth made as they passed through.

Encumbered by the mare, Jess worked to stay with Warner, whose pony scrambled like a dog-harried rabbit through the maze of underbrush. The hours passed slowly as the two riders and three horses made their difficult and hazardous way along mere threads of trails, struggling through the brush.

Dawn glowed softly behind the ridges when Warner found a sheltered spot a little distance upslope to the game trail they had been following.

"We'll wait here a spell, go on at full daylight." he muttered, stepping out of his saddle.

With a chilly feeling along his spine, the feeling that had begun when he spotted the two riders trailing him across the open plains west of Roswell, Jess loosened but did not remove Capitan's saddle. Warner did likewise and tied his cowhorse, then settled down to watch the trail below them.

Jess leaned against a tree. "You think someone took the trail behind us?" he asked Warner softly.

"You never can tell."

"Nothing but a lynx cat could find this trail off the ridge."

"There's more'n one way to get onto the trail. That mare of yours made a hell of a lot of racket in the brush."

Warner's cowpony had done his share of thrashing about in the brush, but Jess let it pass. "Who is it on our trail?"

"Who is it on *your* trail, don't you mean?"

Jess grinned. "I thought maybe I'd lost 'em after I left Lincoln." Briefly he told Warner about the two who had trailed him from Roswell.

"What they after? You got any notion?"

Jess shrugged. "I'd only be guessing."

"Not much you wouldn't. That fancy stud you're riding might be reason enough. That bay stands out like an Irish spud on a prickly pear! There's men would risk bein' staked on a anthill for a mount like—Hold it! Listen!"

Warner got to his feet and drew his gun. Jess eased his Colt from its holster, tracing the sounds that had alerted his companion. Unmistakable, iron clinking on stone, the slow careful thud of a hoofbeat, the soft riffling of a horse's nostrils.

Warner gestured urgently. Jess got to the stud in time to stop the big horse from screaming a challenge to the newcomers. He could not reach the mare, but perhaps she would be more interested in the grass she cropped than in the horses moving now below their hiding place on the narrow trail that overhung the canyon.

There was a sudden clanking of metal. "Damn it to hell!" a muffled voice came to the watchers on the slope. "This plug's gone and pulled a shoe loose."

"See can you get it off him," hissed another voice. "It sounds like a brass band."

Leather creaked. A moment passed. "Okay, I got

it. He'll be tender in a hour in these dad-blamed rocks," muttered the dismounted man.

"We catch up to that Texan we'll both be better mounted. And we'll have the money from that gent in Roswell when we prove we done fer the Texan." He chuckled.

Jess felt quick fury. Abruptly he left the stud and moved, fast and silent, to a low bluff that overlooked the trail just ahead of the riders.

"Just which one of you yellow-bellied polecats is aiming to put me under?" he asked gently.

Incredulous, the two jerked their faces upward to the tall figure crouched on the rocks. Jess had time to see a heavily bearded face under a battered hat, and a rabbit-jawed youngster so thin his wrist bones were more noticeable than the gun he grabbed for.

The older man was fast. His first shot chipped granite near Jess's left shoulder, even as the outlaw whirled his horse on the precarious trail and spurred away, bent low over his *grulla*'s neck. Jess fired, missed, swung his gun to the second target just as Warner's shot bent the spindly youth double.

Even so, the boy managed to fire twice at Jess. The bullets whined by as Jess pulled his trigger. He saw his slug punch the kid's left shoulder. The boy's gun fell at his booted feet, and he toppled into the dirt, moaning and sobbing.

"God almighty, you've killed me! Oh God—"

McClaren scrambled down to the injured outlaw, knelt and turned him over. Warner slid down to the trail. The redhead took one look and shook his head.

"He's done for. Gut shot."

Jess felt cold. Could this have been avoided? If he'd stayed in hiding with Warner, let the horsethieves ride by, might this boy's death have been averted?

But he knew the brutal truth. Waiting would only have given the two opportunity to bushwhack Jess and Warner. There had been little choice, but what there was had been made by the owlhoots, when they took Jess's trail with the persistence of coon hounds. Yet he could take no satisfaction in this outcome. He had never liked the sensation of dealing out death. And this would not be a swift or painless death.

"Oh, Mama, oh Mama." babbled the injured man, blood running from the corner of his mouth. "It hurts. I'm dying. I'm on fire—" His eyes focused on Jess. "Mister, finish it, please!"

Warner looked questioningly at Jess, who shook his head sharply. The cowpuncher shrugged. "Ain't nothing else we can do for him."

"We could get him to a doc."

"Over trails like these? The nearest sawbones is at Fort Stanton—or maybe Doc Potter at Tularosa. Take six, seven hours at least. This scoundrel won't last more'n a few hours at best, less if we move him. It ain't the first gut wound I seen, McClaren. Quilter was shot like that, and he was my friend, but I couldn't do nothin', not even for him. I ain't about to try for this piece of trash. He'd have gunned us both down and laughed about it."

"Gimme my gun," begged the writhing outlaw. "Let me do it. I'll put it to my own head. For God's sake, mister!"

"If you give a gun to this carrion, you are a fool" was Warner's comment, and he moved away to unsaddle and release the boy's horse.

Jess watched the kid on the blood-muddy ground for a sick moment, then found the fallen gun. He placed it in the boy's right hand and turned to climb back to the horses.

"Damn you!" shrieked the fallen gunman. "I'll take you with me to hell!"

"McClaren, look out!" shouted Warner, and simultaneously two shots cracked.

Chapter Three

Something jerked at Jess's denim jacket sleeve. He flung himself to the ground, rolling to come up in a crouch, gun in hand. But there was no need to fire. Mouth open as if still silently spewing hatred, the boy was dead, his upper skull missing. Warner was holstering his gun, his face redder than ever.

"You danged, soft-headed fool! He coulda killed you and me both!"

Jess straightened slowly. "You're right. Sorry, Warner."

"You listen to me," Warner said furiously. "It don't never pay to give a sidewinder no extry chances. It won't buy no posies for your grave!"

"You've said enough. Let's bury him."

"Bury him! This young scorpion wouldn't do no more than leave us for the buzzards, was we in his boots. I hope you ain't forgot he had a pardner, who may be looking down a rifle barrel at us right now." He cast an uneasy look at the morning-misted ridges.

Nevertheless, Jess pulled the body into a gully, piled rocks over him.

"Now," Warner said sourly, "I suppose you'll be wanting to read the Bible over his worthless carcass."

Jess grimaced. "Wouldn't do him much good where he is now."

Warner had brought the horses, the dead boy's flea-bitten gray as well, down to the trail. Swiftly he unsaddled the bushwhacker's mount.

"What brand's he carrying," Jess asked as he tightened the cinch on his own saddle.

"Circle C," Warner grunted. "But I'd bet he's a rented nag. Or stolen. That kid couldn't have bought a burro."

They mounted. Warner took the lead and set a fast pace. He ignored the trails now, spurring his horse down off the mountain to the canyon floor. The cowpony leaped and slid and threaded his way through the dense brush with the agility of an elk.

They followed the creek bed awhile, watchful in case the other bushwhacker might have worked his way ahead of them, then climbed to the next ridge. It was early afternoon before Warner paused for longer than a few minutes to rest the horses. They had crossed seemingly numberless canyons, backtracked to the crest trail for a few miles, and then had taken to the canyons on the west side once more.

Now they sat their horses on a wooded ridge under a lightning-blasted juniper. Nearby, a small bunch of cattle stood with heads and spreading horns lifted, sniffing the wind. Nearly as wild as deer scared up from the brush, the cattle took fright and left at a high, reaching trot.

Warner pointed downcanyon. "That's Whitley's place."

They were looking down upon a collection of corrals and buildings reduced by the distance to toy size. "This here's Venado Canyon. You ride on down. I'll set here a spell, to be sure we wasn't followed."

Jess spoke to the bay and put him to the rocky, winding trail into the valley. He looked back to find Warner's eyes on him, the broad red face screwed into a frown. Apparently the cowhand was still suspicious of McClaren.

Not for the first time Jess wondered what kind of mess he was riding into. He was no stranger to gunplay. Witness the Montwell brothers, laid untimely in their graves. But it was beginning to seem that this entire, vast county was a nest of armed men just aching to throw down on a stranger.

As he put his stud to the descending trail, closely followed by the mare, Jess pondered some questions. If Whitley's trouble had to do with these long-standing Lincoln County frictions Toland had mentioned, why hadn't the rancher joined forces with the other cowmen? Why call in a stranger, even the son of a friend?

And did the dawn attack upon Jess and Warner have anything to do with Whitley's problems? One of the men had said something about being paid by someone in Roswell. Sure would be useful to know that man's name. Not much chance of that. Well, at least he would soon know what Joe Ed Whitley wanted of him.

The bay stepped daintily into the bottom of the canyon. He and the mare drank from the sparkling creek. Slim, white-barked aspen trees were ranked near the stream, along with chokecherry and maples and here and there a mountain ash.

Good water here, Jess noted automatically. But the country as a whole was powder dry. The lower the altitude the more apparent it became that the rains were overdue. Weeds that should have been green and vigorous were as brittle and yellow as in late autumn. In the high canyons, sideoats grama, black grama, and mountain muhly grass still offered adequate forage for cattle. But down there in the wide, distance-hazed basin that stretched for fifty or sixty miles beyond the foothills, there would be scant grass, and less water.

When Capitan and the mare had satisfied their thirst, Jess touched his spurs lightly to the bay's sides, feeling the instant, powerful, response. He rubbed the horse's damp neck. These two horses were all he had in the way of worldly possessions, except for a couple hundred dollars. Ah well, many a man was less fortunate.

McClaren rode the last mile tiredly, letting Capitan choose his own pace. At a wide bend in the canyon, he found the sprawling complex of stables and corrals. Horses in the long, fenced pasture threw their heads up as he approached, calling to McClaren's horses, and raced as near as the wire would allow. Capitan replied shrilly, his big body quivering between Jess's legs.

Jess tied his mare at the corrals, remounted the bay to ride to the ranch house, a large adobe structure with typical Mexican flat roof, *vigas* extending from the upper walls, a *ristra* of long, scarlet peppers glowing against the sand-colored wall. McClaren headed for a big porch on the south side.

He had stepped down and was looping reins over the hitch rail when a voice froze him in his tracks.

"Put your hands up, mister!"

Jess obeyed, startled to see a woman step out onto the porch, her slim, tanned hands competently holding a Henry rifle. She was tall, dressed in a full-skirted blue print dress trimmed with a narrow edge of lace at collar and wrists. Her heavy auburn hair was combed severely off her face, done up in some kind of knot at the back of her head.

McClaren guessed her to be in her early twenties. Large dark eyes were set wide in the slim face, and she might have been pretty if her expression had been less grim.

"Who are you? Say it quickly!" she demanded.

"Jess McClaren. Mr. Joe Ed Whitley sent for me."

Her delicately arched brows drew together. "That's not true. He's sent for no one."

Inwardly Jess cursed Toland's destruction of the letter. "Where is Whitley, miss? He'll vouch for me."

"Where are you from, mister?" she interrupted sharply.

"Austin, Texas. Mr. Whitley wrote to my pa, Morgan McClaren. Ask Mr. Whitley, why don't you?" Jess let his impatience edge his tone.

She seemed in the grip of indecision. "Joe Ed knows no one in Austin, Texas," she asserted.

Jess clamped a lid on his temper. His arms were beginning to ache from being held skyward.

"You sure of that? Whitley and Morgan McClaren were at Gettysburg together."

Her chin lifted stubbornly. "Then why isn't your pa here, instead of you?"

"Mr. Whitley sent for me. And my pa is dead."

Jess felt the angry impulse to get on the bay and ride out. Never in his life had he been treated with such suspicion, even by chance-met strangers, as here in Lincoln County. The pleasure of being held at gunpoint was wearing thin. He was almighty tempted to get on his horse and just keep going—providing the girl would let him leave in one piece.

"Look, lady," he snapped. "If Mr. Whitley don't

want me here after all, he can tell me so. I ain't particularly anxious to stay where I'm not wanted."

"How'd you find this ranch? You came by the upper trail!" she accused, bewilderingly. "A stranger wouldn't know that way in."

"I was guided by a man who says he works for Whitley. He's nearly as suspicious as you are." Jess's voice was wry. "Name of Red Warner. Ugly, bad-tempered—maybe you'd ought to git him down here and question him along with me."

"Where's Red now?"

He told her, angrier with every word. In another instant he was going to have to take that gun away from her, at some risk to both of them.

Abruptly she lowered the rifle barrel. "Wait here," she said coldly, and slipped back into the house.

Jess lowered his aching arms and finished securing his horse. The stallion was restless, jerking at his reins and stamping at the iron-hard earth.

The young woman reappeared, rifle held downward. "All right. You can come in."

At her gesture, Jess went ahead of her, blinking in the shadowed dimness of a big room with exposed beams and a fireplace at one end, Navajo rugs like splashes of soft, colored light on the pine floor. There was heavy, Mexican-made furniture of stout dark wood and leather, a clutter of lariats, rifles, braided-leather quirts, and long-roweled spurs hanging on wall pegs.

"Straight ahead, into the next room, then to your right."

Jess walked through a dining room, then into a hallway and toward the back of the house. At the last door, she stopped him.

"Go in, but very quietly. If Mr. Whitley knows you, you can stay."

Now what the devil did she mean by that? McClaren pushed open the door and stepped inside.

A bedroom. White muslin curtains fluttered at open windows. Massive mahogany bureau and chest of drawers, a big bed with heavy, carved head- and footboards.

And in the bed, a man. Whitley?

Uncertainly, reminded of days not long past when

he had bent over his father's bed, Jess approached. The gray-haired man's strong, big-boned face was quiet, eyes shut.

"Mr. Whitley?" Jess said quietly.

The eyes opened at once, and there was a sudden movement of the sick man's right hand, as if he instinctively groped for a gun.

"Mr. Whitley, I'm Jess McClaren, Morgan's son. You sent for me."

Alertly the man's dark eyes searched Jess's face. "Morgan's boy!" he muttered.

"Yes sir. You wrote to my pa—"

This seemed to irritate him. "I remember! I ain't clean gone in the head yet," he said in a hoarse, breathless voice. "Been—waiting for you. Will you help a old man out, son?"

The direct, unapologetic question reminded Jess of Morgan. "Never beat around the bush," he used to say. "It only wastes good time."

Now Jess nodded. "I'll help if I can, sir. Pa's told me often what you did for him. I owe you, for his sake."

Whitley waved a hand weakly to brush away the reminder of past actions. "Maggie!" Surprisingly, it was a roar.

She entered the room and came at once to his side. Seeing the rifle still in her hand, Whitley grinned. Jess felt an instant liking for the old man.

"Ain't taking no chances, are you, Maggie girl?"

"What is it, Joe Ed? You shouldn't be yelling that way," she scolded anxiously, setting the gun aside.

"This man here. Give him anything he wants. He's a friend—" He struggled suddenly for breath. Deftly Maggie lifted his head. She held a water glass to the rancher's bluish lips, let him sip slowly. Whitley laid his head back.

"Rest now, Joe Ed," the woman said firmly. "I'll see to Mr. McClaren."

She shooed Jess from the room, followed after, closing the door quietly.

"I owe you an apology," she said bluntly.

He shrugged. "I'd rather have a cup of coffee, if you can spare it."

"Come into the kitchen."

"I'd best see to my horses first."

She shook her head, her glance cool. "I'll have someone do that. Come."

He followed her, noting the way she moved, her body slender and graceful, strength and decision in every step. He wondered why she pinned up the beautiful mass of her hair in such an unappealing way.

The kitchen was large, sunny. Near the big black range a trim, attractive woman tilted her head curiously. She had shining dark braids wound about her head, and black eyes, and must once have been a woman to set a man's pulse pounding. Another woman, with pale gold hair, was brewing tea in a china pot. She, too, stared at Jess.

"Manuela," Maggie said. "Have you anything to make a meal, quickly?"

"*Sí.*" The dark woman nodded. "I have the *frijoles,* and there is venison roasted." She turned energetically and went into an adjacent pantry.

"Maggie, who is this man?" asked the second woman. She was not as tall as Maggie. McClaren guessed her to be in her forties, but she was still a good-looking woman. Her eyes were blue, with a look of shrewd intelligence. Her thin, high-bridged nose and elegantly lifted head were arresting, as was the fine-grained white skin, rare in a land where the sun browned everyone, sooner or later.

At the stove, Maggie lifted a granite-ware coffeepot, touched the side to see if it was hot, and poured black fragrant coffee into a thick cup. She brought the cup to the scrubbed plank table in the center of the room.

"Anna." She turned to the blond woman. "This is Mr. Jess McClaren. He will be staying for a time. Mr. McClaren, Mrs. Whitley."

The blonde ignored the introduction. "Why?" she said, with clear hostility. By now Jess would have been astonished by a friendlier greeting.

"He is here visiting Joe Ed."

"I repeat, why?"

Jess dropped his hat on the table and sat down to take up the coffee. Be damned if he was going to explain himself to anyone else. He kept his face expressionless as Maggie continued her explanation, her voice cool and brisk.

"Mr. McClaren's father was an old friend. Mr. McClaren is passing through Lincoln County and dropped in to pay his respects. Joe Ed has asked him to stay on for a time."

Not quite the truth, and why not, Miss Maggie? Jess wondered, swallowing coffee.

"I see," Anna replied. "Then you will be moving on very soon?" She pinned Jess with her rather round, pale eyes.

Apparently, Mrs. Whitley liked visitors about as much as everyone else in Lincoln County.

Jess gazed back at her blandly. "My plans are indefinite, Mrs. Whitley. I appreciate Mr. Whitley's invitation."

"Mr. Whitley is very ill, Mr.—"

"McClaren," Jess supplied, eyeing her.

"My husband is scarcely able to entertain guests."

"Joe Ed insisted," Maggie put in quietly. "You know how he is when he's set his heart on something." Jess had the feeling that she disliked defending him, and he was amused.

"We'll give Mr. McClaren the room next to Joe Ed's," Maggie added.

Whitley's wife let the subject rest. With another sharp glance in Jess's direction, she left the kitchen.

Jess met Maggie's unsmiling eyes. "What was that all about?"

"Anna can be rude." She flushed, and he suspected that she had reminded herself that *she* hadn't been exactly welcoming.

Manuela returned to the kitchen with a plate of cold sliced meat. She ladled beans onto the plate, adding a slice of fresh bread from the loaves cooling on a shelf near the open window. The food tasted wonderful. Jess had to restrain himself from eating too fast, one of the rules his ma had drilled into him as a boy.

Maggie excused herself. "I'll be in the garden when you finish. Manuela will show you," she said.

Moments later Jess was startled to see his stud lope past the kitchen windows toward the stables, Maggie astride the saddle. Her skirts were hiked up to her boot tops, showing a petticoat ruffle trimmed with lace—the first hint of feminine softness he'd noticed about Maggie. She rode with natural grace. Jess wondered what the stallion thought about those skirts flapping in his flank. He'd never been ridden by a woman, and his head was nervously high, ears laid back as if he contemplated some drastic action. Maggie ignored the peevish warning and gigged the big bay with her heels, letting him line out in a run.

Jess got up to watch from the back door, somewhat relieved to see that Maggie kept the horse in control.

He went back to his meal, complimenting Manuela on her cooking. She smiled her pleasure and refilled his coffee cup.

The back door opened and a boy of five or so came in.

"Manuela, I'm hungry!" he announced, but his eyes, wide with curiosity, were glued upon Jess.

The boy was fair-haired, eyes brown. Freckles sprinkled his sunburned nose, and his square small hands were grubby.

"*Madre de Dios!*" Manuela exclaimed, throwing up her hands. "You have already had *su comida*."

"He's eating," said the child, pointing sternly to Jess. "I want some of Maggie's bread. I smelled it cooking."

Muttering with mock despair, Manuela sliced bread and spread it with molasses from a tin bucket. "Now go out and play. *Andale!*"

"No. I want to talk to that man." He crawled into a chair and regarded Jess solemnly from the opposite end of the table. He bit into the soft bread and chewed, still studying McClaren. A string of dark syrup adorned his chin.

"Mister, who are you?" he asked.

"My name is McClaren." Jess chewed a bite of venison with appreciation. These were the most comfortable few minutes he'd known in many days. Now if he could manage for a wash and change of dusty clothing.

"I'm Joey," said the child, licking a mud-and-molasses-coated finger. "I don't know you."

Jess grinned. "Wellsir, reckon I don't know you, either."

Joey thought about this in silence, rapidly consuming the sticky bread. "Does Maggie know you're here?" he demanded. "She ain't gonna like it." His look was earnest. It seemed to be a friendly warning.

"She knows. Is Maggie your sister?"

The boy blinked as if amazed at such ignorance. "No sir! Maggie's my ma. I don't want any sisters!"

Startled, Jess studied him. There was a hint of Maggie's slim face in Joey's round one. The eyes were alike, wide-set, clear, coffee-dark.

Manuela seemed suddenly flustered. Quickly she lifted the little boy from his chair, scolding in a rapid mixture of Spanish and English, and shooed him out the back door.

Jess stood and thanked the woman for the meal. "That hit the spot, Manuela. I was lank as a dogie calf."

"De nada, señor." She nodded gravely. She told him how to find the garden. He stepped out the back door.

Maggie's vegetable patch was toward the stables, along the creek. Jess stepped over the fence and removed his Stetson as she straightened from yanking weeds.

"Pretty dry times for a garden," he observed.

She glanced at her plants, frowning. "Yes. I've been carrying water from the creek. But it's not the same as rain. Nothing grows as well."

"I met your son, Mrs.—" Jess hesitated, realizing he didn't know the name.

She turned to face him swiftly, and he was reminded of some small, vulnerable animal suddenly cornered.

"My name is Maggie Bourne, Mr. McClaren," she said.

"Mrs. Bourne." He nodded.

"No." Color rose in her face. Her hands were very still. "You might as well hear it now," she said icily. "You will, soon enough. Bourne was my father's name. I'm not Mrs. anything."

Jess felt embarrassed at blundering into a private matter. "I'm sorry, ma'am. I didn't mean to—"

"You have nothing to apologize for," she snapped, bending to grasp a sunflower and uproot it from a row of corn.

Jess searched for something to say. "Seems like I came at a bad time. What's wrong with Mr. Whitley?"

"He's been sick for a long time, but none of us knew it," the girl said bitterly. "It's his heart, the doctor says. Joe Ed had a very bad spell a couple of weeks ago, when Mac Quilter was killed from ambush. Joe Ed hired Mac when he was fourteen, years ago. Mac thought of Mr. Whitley as a father, as I do."

She seemed to expect the questioning look in Jess's eyes. "Joe Ed took me in when I was a baby. My folks were passing through Tularosa and took sick of the smallpox. They died. Mr. Whitley raised me as his own. I owe Joe Ed everything."

Jess noticed that she did not include Anna Whitley in her statement of gratitude.

"Whitley had no children of his own, I suppose," he remarked, for something to say.

"You suppose wrong, Mr. McClaren!" She turned away abruptly. "He has a son, Daniel."

"Then maybe this Daniel is the man I should see. I need to find out what Mr. Whitley had in mind when he sent for me."

She was moving swiftly along the row of corn, bending gracefully. Her long, tanned fingers sought out and destroyed weeds with a kind of violent satisfaction.

"Daniel's been gone from the ranch some six years. I've no idea where he is—or even if he's still alive."

"Then maybe you can tell me what I need to know."

She straightened, staring across the wide canyon to the ridges beyond. "I didn't even know you'd been sent for."

"But you must have some idea what the trouble is."

She turned abruptly back to him, her wide dark eyes cool and intent. Loosened strands of hair curled at her temples. Jess realized that this woman could be beautiful, if she cared to be.

"Mr. McClaren, exactly what was in the letter Mr. Whitley wrote to your pa?"

He told her, as nearly as he could remember, explaining that Toland had destroyed the note. She nodded as if this did not surprise her.

"And are you good with a gun?"

He shrugged, not liking the question. "I ain't looking to put it out for hire, if that's what you mean. I can defend myself, I reckon, in fair fight."

She examined him with narrowed eyes, as a man would study a horse to see if he was sound before buying him. McClaren felt irritated, knowing what kind of picture he presented: dusty, ragged, thin, like a man on the run.

"You'd defend the man who hired you? No matter the odds?"

He thought this a stupid question, and his mouth thinned. "I could, and I would. But somebody might trouble to tell me why Mr. Whitley needs defending."

She shook her head impatiently. "We've had stock run off, a lot more than we can afford to lose. There's always some minor rustling. We lose a steer now and again to the dry farmers on the flats. They're going under, with the drought. Soon they'll be forced out. Joe Ed never has begrudged a beef to a man who can't feed his family. He knows most of the farmers, and he warned them when they came and put the first plow to the grass that the wet years were rare. Still he respects them for having the courage to try."

"The rustling is more than just a few head taken by the settlers?"

"Red Warner can tell you more accurately, but I've ridden this spread with Joe Ed since I was a little girl, and I'd estimate that a third of the cows are missing, since spring."

Jess gave a low whistle. "Whitley's got no idea who's behind it?"

She shook her head. "Red and Curly Brissom watch

the herds as well as they can. We're short-handed since Mac was killed. Joe Ed and I rode every day and some nights, until he got sick. Now, I can't leave him."

She seemed to go inward, absently rubbing her forehead, leaving a streak of garden soil there. It made her seem younger, someone to be protected. Then he thought of Maggie, greeting him with rifle in hand, and repressed a grin. This lady needed protection about as much as a porcupine.

"None of you ever spotted anything?" he asked.

"Joe Ed and Mac trailed the thieves once, caught them driving the cows past Wildy Wells. That's south of here, way beyond our range. The rustlers spotted them and started shooting, then left the cows and ran for it. Joe Ed and Quilter got a look at the thieves, but they weren't from around here. One of them was hit, knocked off his horse. His partner took him on behind his saddle."

"Too bad he couldn't have been held and questioned," Jess mused. "Is there any particular reason cow thieves work this spread more than others?"

Her look was anxious. "I don't know. Joe Ed has a good supply of water, and enough grass to keep his cows alive, or so we hope, until the rains come. Some of the other ranchers are in bad shape. In the high country, or where wells are holding out, the stock fares better. But more wells dry up all the time. Someone could be hoping to get hold of J-bar-W's water and graze."

"That could mean a neighboring ranch is in it."

She shook her head. "We're bordered on the north by Clear River Ranch. They aren't that short of water, though we hear they're suffering some. Pardue is south. He's hurting for water, but Joe Ed has never minded to share with him. We've known Mr. Pardue for years, and trusted him as he trusts us. I can't believe he'd try to ruin Joe Ed."

Jess realized suddenly that he was bone-tired. "Uh . . . could you point me to the bunkhouse, Miss Bourne?" He ran a hand over his dusty beard. "I could do with a wash, I expect."

"You're to stay at the house. I'll have Manuela heat water for you."

All business again, she dusted her hands, and led the way to the ranch house.

Chapter Four

After vigorous use of hot water and hard yellow soap and the last clean shirt from his saddlebags had improved his travel-worn appearance, Jess inspected himself in the dresser mirror. Maggie Bourne had shown him to a large airy room on the cool north side of the house. It was as comfortable a place as any he'd ever known. It was furnished with dark, massive Mexican furniture, with snowy linen scarves on the dresser and chest of drawers and not a speck of dust anywhere. It was enough to make a man damned uneasy.

Manuela had called a slim youth, a smiling boy she introduced as Concepcion, one of her two sons, to bring in a wooden tub and help her with cans of hot water. Jess would have been satisfied with a pitcher and basin, but resignedly made use of the luxury offered him.

His damp hair and beard resisted combing, and he reflected that he'd better borrow a pair of scissors from the cook and do some trimming.

His faded check shirt was wrinkled but clean. There was nothing much he could do about his pants. They'd about seen their day. He'd have to buy another pair the first chance he got.

It occurred abruptly to him that he was doing an almighty lot of worrying about clothes and haircuts. He wasn't here to play the part of town dandy.

Someone tapped at his door. Hastily he gathered up

dirty clothes and thrust them out of sight before opening the door.

It was the boy, Joey, his eyes red and puffy.

"Maggie says tell you come to supper," he announced somberly.

"Tell your ma I'll eat with the help. Where's the cook shack?"

"Everbody eats in the kitchen. Grampa says nobody not good enough to eat with the family ain't good enough to ride for him." Joey snuffled and rubbed at his eyes.

"Something wrong, son?" McClaren asked.

Joey swallowed hard. "My horny toad, he fell outta my pocket in the corral, and one of them horses stepped on 'im."

Tears started to roll down his cheeks again as he related the disaster. He wiped his nose on his sleeve, straightened his shoulders manfully. "But it ain't nothing, though," he assured Jess.

"Makes a man feel low when he loses something special like that," Jess said.

"Yessir," choked Joey. "Maggie says you come and eat right away."

The kitchen seemed crowded. Men were already seated around the table. Red Warner nodded at Jess as he came in. Across from him a cowboy with a head of thin, curly brown hair and a drooping mustache was spearing a slab of steak. Manuela's sons grinned at Jess as Joey tugged him to a chair next to his own.

"Boys, this here's Jess McClaren," said Red. "McClaren, meet Curly Brissom And that there's José, and Concepcion."

Jess acknowledged the introductions.

"Might be McClaren will be ridin' some with us," Warner continued, with an inquiring look at Jess.

Jess nodded and took a steak from the platter. He accepted the big crockery bowl of *frijoles* that was making the rounds, steadying it for Joey, who ladled a monster helping onto his plate and dug in, apparently drowning his grief in good hot food.

Manuela brought hot flour tortillas and passed a

dish of yellow butter. Jess whistled in surprise and appreciation.

"We have a cow for the *leche,*" Manuela explained proudly.

This was unheard of luxury. Most ranchers thought milk cows were for dirt farmers and wouldn't fool with one. Jess applauded J-bar-W's break with tradition as he bit into the buttered tortilla.

He found himself glancing about for Maggie. Neither she nor Mrs. Whitley was in the room, but then he could scarcely picture the dainty blond Anna eating with cowhands.

Manuela poured coffee for Jess, leaning near. "Miss Margarita is with Señor Whitley," she murmured. "After supper he will talk with you."

Jess nodded, conscious of Red Warner's speculative glance as he overheard the message.

Maggie was leaving Mr. Whitley's room when Jess came along the hall.

"Is he well enough to talk?" Jess asked.

She sighed. "No, Mr. McClaren, but he insists, and gets upset if I try to prevent it. Please don't stay long, and don't excite him."

"Ma'am, I'll do my best." He went into the bedroom. The rancher was propped up in bed and looked slightly better than he had earlier in the day. He gestured McClaren to a chair near the bed.

"How is your pa, son? I ain't seen him in a coon's age."

"He's gone, Mr. Whitley. I got your letter just after we buried him."

Whitley shook his head. "I'm right sorry to hear that. We was good friends, though it'd been years since we last shook hands. I reckon you're wondering why I sent for you."

"Miss Bourne tells me you've had cow thieves. We had some of the same breed of coyotes working our herds down in the cedar brakes. Some of the ranchers were nearly wiped out. We finally tracked the varmints down."

Whitley looked grim. "I gotta do the same here.

Won't be the first time I held what's mine against renegades and scoun'ls. But there's more to it than that."

Whitley paused, scowling, as Jess waited quietly. At last the old man continued.

"Goes against my grain to whine, son, but somebody has it in for me. Maggie don't know it, and nor does anyone but Red, but twice somebody tried to pot me from ambush. Rifle fire."

Jess frowned. "Unless you came on the thieves at work, why would ordinary rustlers draw a bead on you?"

"That's what's teasin' my brain, an' I cain't come up with a good answer. For years now there's been many a little bunch o' cows drove over the Rio Grande. It's said some don't go that far, but is butchered and sold to the fort and the hides buried. Generally the polecats who sneak the steers off a man's range ain't got the stomach fer murder, though. The money's all they care about."

He stopped, visibly tiring.

"You got enemies, Mr. Whitley?"

The old rancher shook his head. "Not to my knowledge. Most everybody eats somebody else's beef. Me and my family never have. I don't take what someone else has worked for. I've kep' my word with all men."

A thought struck Jess, and he leaned forward. "Mr. Whitley, it's gonna take every pair of eyes we can trust to get to the bottom of this. We'll have to patrol at night, have riders out as much as possible. I'm told you have a son. Shouldn't you send for him, and anyone else who maybe owes you a favor?"

Whitley's face went stony. "You been told wrong, McClaren. I got no son." Abruptly he turned his head away. "I'll talk to you later," he mumbled.

Puzzled, Jess left the room, got his hat, and sought out Red Warner. He was seated on a bench in front of the bunk house, whistling tunelessly and whittling at a length of stove wood.

Before McClaren could speak, Warner gestured to the tall man to follow him and led him out of hearing of anyone inside the log bunkhouse.

He leaned against a pole corral. Inside, McClaren's

bay stud contentedly chewed prairie hay. Warner spat tobacco. "What's on your mind, McClaren?"

"Whitley thinks someone is out to ruin him, maybe put him under for good. Says he's been shot at twice."

"That's so."

"But if he has any ideas who's behind it, he ain't saying. Miss Bourne told me about the owlhoots Quilter and Whitley caught with J-bar-W cows."

Warner nodded shortly.

"Miss Bourne says they were strangers."

"The country's crawling with yahoos who don't mind a little trip south of the border with stolen beef. They could have been working on their own."

"But you don't think so."

Red gave him a penetrating look, and shrugged.

Jess persisted. "Did they see anything that day that makes Whitley suspect someone local is settin' in on the game?"

Warner hesitated, then spoke slowly and with a care to his words. "Ask Joe Ed. He was there."

"He's a sick man," McClaren said. "I don't like to upset him more than I have to. He's asked me for help, and I aim to do whatever I can—but I can't do no good ridin' blind."

"Wellsir." Warner stirred uneasily. "I'll tell you, but don't think I'm making any accusations. They just ain't enough to go on, and it ain't the smartest thing in the world for me to shoot off my mouth."

"I'll keep whatever you say to myself."

"Quilter said one of them saddle tramps was riding a circle-P cowhorse. Old man Pardue hisself used to ride that paint. Flashy horse, lots of black to the body and head, white stocking legs, some splashes of white on both sides."

"You ask this man Pardue about it?"

Warner chuckled, not with amusement. "Nobody asks that kind of questions hereabouts."

"What about the law?"

"Sheriff Ascarate?" Warner shrugged. "Well, he ain't a bad sort, once you git to know him. But he's in Las Cruces. Mostly he *stays* in Las Cruces, as the climate is definitely unhealthy in the Tularosa flats and these here mountains."

"Maggie—Miss Bourne seems to think Pardue can be trusted. Maybe the horse was stolen."

"It's back in the circle-P remuda now. Joe Ed took a little *pasear* over that way and checked, one evening late. Said he saw the paint plain as day. But that still don't mean much. They'd winged the man riding him, knocked him outta the saddle. His buddy took him up behind. The horse was running scared, likely headed for home. Doubtless it'd been stolen in the first place, and fer damn sure ol' man Pardue is smart enough to *say* the horse was stolen. It don't leave us nowhere."

"I'd like to look over the J-bar-W as soon as I can, get to know my way around," Jess told him.

"We can start in the morning. Takes a good two weeks to git over all the spread, rough as the upper canyons are, but we can ride the boundaries in three, four days."

Dawn was still only a promise when Jess threw his saddle on the back of a J-bar-W dun. The horse had a white-ringed eyeball and little ears laid back flat, and he wrung his tail irritably when Jess pulled the cinch tight and stepped on. Feeling the hump in the pony's back, Jess sighed and yanked his hat down. He gave the horse the slack he was waiting for to get his head down, and was ready when the first skyward escalation came.

The dun gelding hit the ground with pile-driver legs and launched himself again into the air, kicking high behind.

Jess leaned far back and raked the gelding's shoulders and neck with spur rowels, digging just hard enough for encouragement. Fitting his lean body to the dun's violent, twisting action, he balanced in the precarious saddle, he and the horse the center of a choking cloud of dirt that circled the corral like a wind-spiraled dust devil.

When the dun showed signs of boredom with the early morning exercise, Jess spurred him again and slapped the steep rump with his hat, producing a couple of halfhearted jumps. He pulled the dun to a heaving stop near Warner's mount.

Red was grinning. "Joe Ed would have relished seeing that," he said. "He likes his horses with a lot of fight and he likes the man who ain't afraid to let 'em do their worst."

Jess let Warner lead off from the corral. Red headed for the north ridge, climbing at a steep slant. The horses struck a patiently laboring trot over a rocky thread of a trail to the crest. On the grassy ridge, they let the horses catch their wind. Jess looked eastward over the tangle of forested canyons and distant peaks gilded by the sunrise. It was a wild, beautiful country, but must be hell on horses and men during roundups. They were far above the treeline here, though a few stunted, twisted cedars and piñons had hung on. It seemed to Jess that on these high ridges the wind would touch earth for the first time ever—certainly the air here was as pure and sweet as any a man would ever taste. He judged that snow would stack ten or twelve feet deep in a normal winter. Even now, when the surface of the ground was cracking for want of rain, mountain bunch grass stood high as a horse's knee. But mostly it was last year's growth, dry and yellow.

Westward, Venado Canyon still lay in shadow, and would for an hour or more. The great basin beyond was tinted rose and yellow in the new light. Warner pointed out the thick, ragged black line that was the ancient lava flow of the Mal Pais beginning some seventy miles north. In strange contrast, the White Sands rolled from the south and west to meet the gigantic lava beds.

McClaren had heard of the Sands, of the outlandish beauty of this freak of nature. The miles of pale dunes were the haunt of rattler and coyote. Only the most stubborn desert vegetation could gain a hold out there. It was a wasteland, but savagely fascinating.

Beyond the barrier of the Sands and the Mal Pais, Jess could see the blue, serrated line of the next mountain ranges. Red named them for him: the San Andres, the Oscuras, and southward, the Organs.

Warner reached in his shirt pocket for a plug of tobacco and bit off a chew. "Yonder's Mockingbird Gap." He nodded toward a distant notch in the San

Andres. "Through there you run into the Jornado del Muerto. Bad country. Ain't nobody likes it but Apaches and fellers on the run."

He spurred his bay and led the way down a narrow ridge to the east. There was little, if any, trail "It ain't so easy to bushwhack a man if he's on the highest place around," he remarked. "Most riders use the canyon trails. They're easier. They're in rifle range of any sharpshooter waitin' on a bluff, too. I ride the ridges, mostly."

He showed McClaren the canyons on the east side where J-bar-W cows ran, along with strays of other brands. In this vast territory, undivided by fences, cows mingled as freely as their bovine minds gave them the urge. Seasonal roundups worked by representatives—"reps"—from the various ranches brought the herds together for the purpose of cutting out individual owners' calves for branding, or steers to be driven to the railhead.

A generous portion of the east slopes and canyons was J-bar-W land. Below and further east there were small holdings of settlers and farmers.

On the west side of the divide five major canyons were Whitley's property: Spur, Venado, Evening Star, Black Bear, and Apache. North of Apache lay other ranches, among them the Clear River spread.

J-bar-W's winter pastures extended far out into the Tularosa Basin. By late afternoon Warner and McClaren were back on the crest, overlooking these areas. They made camp—a concealed one—with a tiny fire that Red doused as soon as their coffee was made.

"I'll keep first watch," McClaren offered, but Red shook his head. "No need. These cowponies will nicker if a rider comes close, an' no one travels these ridges afoot. Take your ease. I'm a light sleeper."

McClaren didn't mention it, but he was not known for heavy slumber either, and he came awake in an instant when Red left his blankets an hour before dawn and moved quietly away into the brush. Call of nature, McClaren thought, and dozed again. He came sharply awake when Red's soft footfalls reentered the little, off-the-ridge clearing. Jess rolled out. Dawn was streaking the east.

"You were gone awhile," he commented. "Cutting for sign?"

Warner gave him a glance before he bent to gather some kindling. "Yeah." He grinned. "We was guarded by angels, I reckon. Not even a bobcat track out there."

They cooked bacon and beans, washed it down with black coffee, then quickly saddled the horses. By full sunup they were beginning to move westward down the serpentine spine of a ridge to the flatland. It was a two-hour ride, though they could push the horses a bit faster when they reached the foothills.

At last they were moving out into the Tularosa Basin, and out here the drought could be seen in all its power. What grass was left from the early summer growth was brittle, burned by heat and drought. There was no moisture and little sustenance in it for cow or horse. The sand was powder dry, and dust rose at each hoof fall. The men rode at a steady trot, making only one brief stop to rest their mounts as the day wore on, baking hot.

J-bar-W had two dug wells topped by wooden towers and windmills. The men camped at the first of these, relieved to find a finger-breadth stream of water being lifted into the rock-and-mortar water tank. A bony, wide-horned steer drifted in to drink, sucking up the water as fast as it was pumped. With nightfall, the hot, dry wind vanished and the mill creaked to a halt. Rolled in his blanket, Jess lay awake listening to the mill's ponderous swiveling as the short-lived breezes tantalized it. This was not his land, nor were the cattle his, but he knew the anguish of the stockmen as they waited for rain that did not fall, knowing that their herds were doomed if relief did not come soon.

The next day was as hot as any Jess had known in Texas. In the stockman's instinctive way, he scanned the horizon for promising clouds. Nothing. The sky hung over them, as hard and blue as if made of cunningly painted stone.

They rode mostly in silence, jogging over the hot, arid flats where each mesquite, greasewood, and cactus occupied its own red hummock of sand. and the horses were forced to weave in and out among the growth.

When they stopped, dismounting and loosening the cinches for a few minutes, impulse made McClaren ask, "What can you tell me about Mr. Whitley's son?"

Warner sent a sharp glance his way. "Why do you want to know?"

Jess shrugged. "Seems to me he's the one ought to be here trying to help his pa."

"Danny Whitley wouldn't take a extry breath to help Joe Ed."

"Why?"

"Ruckus several years back. Joe Ed run Daniel off the place. Told him never to come back."

"Why?" McClaren asked again. Maybe Warner wouldn't tell him, but it was worth a try.

Warner lifted his hat and wiped dirt and sweat off his forehead with his shirtsleeve. "Maybe you might as well know, so you don't go mentioning Daniel's name around the family," he muttered. "But keep it to yourself, if you want to stay popular."

"I can keep my mouth shut."

"You've seen Miss Maggie's little boy. Wellsir, Danny Whitley is that boy's pa. An' that's why Joe Ed run his own son off the ranch, and that's why you don't talk about Danny around J-bar-W."

Jess stared at Warner, who pointedly changed the subject. "She's a dry country!" He spat a stream of tobacco into the red dust. "Most men's cows is already sickening for water. We're lucky to have grass and water left up high."

They rode south most of that day, then turned east again, camping in the foothills. The air was cooler here as night fell, and the fourth day's ride up Dead Man's Ridge to the crest and north again to Venado was more pleasant. They saw more cows in the higher reaches of the J-bar-W. Most were in tolerable shape and the calves looked good. But Jess had the feeling that there were fewer bunches of stock than he ought to be seeing.

As they neared Venado Canyon, the dun Jess was

riding brushed a clump of high grass. A rattler shattered the quiet with its spine-chilling threat. The ground moved in a sinuous band among the stems of grass.

Jess's gun was in his hand, the shot smashing the ugly, triangular head of the snake almost before his gelding had finished a sidewise leap.

Warner whistled in admiration. "You're fast, McClaren. I hope you're as good with the two-legged variety of serpent. But I guess you are good enough to earn your pay."

McClaren's eyes narrowed. "Get this straight, Warner. I ain't a hired gun."

Red shrugged. "No offense. I just figured Joe Ed had sent out for artillery. It ain't all that uncommon, hereabouts, though Whitley would have been too durned proud in his younger days to give *his* snake killin' into other hands."

Jess was not pacified. "I came here to pay off a debt. I'll do all I can to help Mr. Whitley. But no man can point out another to me and set me on his trail like a hunting dog. If I draw this gun, I'll have a damn good reason."

Warner shrugged and spurred his tired horse on.

It was near dark when they unsaddled their tired horses in the corral at J-bar-W headquarters.

"Hey, Red," greeted Curly, who was running a brush over McClaren's stud. "I checked on them cows and calves up on the Evenin' Star water. Drove 'em up in the brush to make it harder for anyone to gather 'em."

"See anything outta the way?"

"Horse tracks, made last day or two. None of us been up in there."

"Might be a good place to watch, come dark," McClaren suggested.

"Tonight?"

"Why not?"

Red appeared to consider it. He shrugged. "Well, caint do any harm, I reckon."

Curly stood back from the bay. "Say, McClaren, where'd you get this horse? I'd give a year's wages for one half as good. Or that black mare, either. She is a looker. You figuring to start a horse herd for yourself?"

"When I get settled down. Maybe up in Colorado."

Curly grinned. "You ought to latch on to a rich wife, or one with land of her own. Now you take Miss Maggie, for instance. Wouldn't surprise me, she'll own half of this spread someday, and she ain't half bad. Man if she'd just look at me twice—"

"I don't reckon we need to discuss Miss Bourne." Jess's voice was icy.

Curly bristled, but Warner stepped in before he could argue. "Let's go in to supper."

Manuela was just setting the inevitable crockery bowl of *frijoles* on the table when Red and Jess stepped on the back porch to wash in the basin. The water in the bucket was pleasantly cool, but the best the men could do was cut the layers of dust on hands and faces.

McClaren rolled up the sleeves of his shirt, remembering that he needed to find out about having his clothes washed. He asked Warner, who was spluttering as he splashed water on his face.

"Give 'em to Manuela. She washes everbody's duds. I pay her a quarter a week."

Jess reached for the yellow bar of homemade lye soap and worked it into a dubious lather between hard palms, then scrubbed face and neck and up to his elbows.

He threw the wash water into the backyard and poured fresh for rinsing, throwing that away in turn. Red handed him the rough-woven towel.

Maggie did not appear for supper. Manuela explained that the girl and José had driven into Tularosa to do some shopping that morning and would be back before nightfall.

McClaren looked up from his steak to ask "How's Mr. Whitley feeling?"

"Oh, he is better! He says he is hungry as a coyote in winter." Manuela laughed and brought the big coffeepot to the table to refill the men's cups.

Red leaned over. "McClaren, if it's all right with you, we'll ride out at full dark."

"Sure." He rose from the table, waving away a third helping of Manuela's rhubarb pie. "Meet you at the corral in a few minutes."

He was as good as his word, having fetched an extra

box of shells from his saddlebags in his room and put on his denim jacket. It would be cold at this altitude as the night progressed, and there would be little opportunity to move around to warm himself after the watch began.

He paused to check the load of his Colt and left the house by the back way.

Chapter Five

Warner and Curly were already saddling up. "You want I should rope you out a mount?" Curly asked.

"Anyone care if I use that gray?" McClaren nodded toward a tall, rangy mare with a Roman nose, among the seven or eight saddle horses Concepcion had herded in. He liked the way the mare's legs were set well under and ready for action, and the slope of her shoulder promised a nice gait. Her withers were prominent enough to keep a saddle in place.

Warner chuckled. "You're sure welcome to her. No one but Joe Ed hisself ever rides that hellion. However, I'd sure like to see you try. She ain't been rode for some months."

McClaren's rope snaked over the heads of the milling cowhorses. The gray ducked, and he was obliged to make a second loop. It fell accurately this time, and in moments Jess had adjusted a bridle with a spade-roller bit to fit the gray's unattractive head and was throwing his blanket and saddle on the mare's back.

She stood quiet as you please until Jess landed in the saddle, then she proceeded to dish up her own brand of Hades for McClaren.

The gray had tricks the dun gelding had never thought of. McClaren had put in a long day. The sunfishing, spinning animal had a devious way of coming to earth with a tremendous jolt and immediately ducking back under her rider, making it damned hard to sit in the saddle. McClaren was tossed onto the saddle horn, a painfully distracting mishap, and then dislodged. He hit the ground full length, just managing to roll away from the mare's hooves.

He stood, grinning and shaking his head. Red handed him his hat, then caught the gray and held her ready for the second go-round. There were anticipatory smiles on Red and Curly's faces as McClaren's boot toe hit the left stirrup and the gray erupted off the ground.

Jess found the saddle, got his balance, and with a quick movement raked his unwilling mount fore and aft with his spur rowels.

The indignant mare bawled like a new-branded calf, snaked her long neck and ugly head groundward, and got down to serious business.

But McClaren was onto her secret weapon now. With a savage joy he matched himself to the pounding, jolting, kicking action, and rode the gray to a stand-still.

Curly Brissom let out a whoop and threw his old hat on the ground. "Now that was a *ride*!"

Warner mounted as Curly opened the corral gate. The three men rode out into the night.

It was over an hour before they reached the Evening Star water, a spring-fed pool about midway down a long canyon. The men stationed themselves on the north slope, overlooking the water hole.

The moon was well up. McClaren could see the shapes of cows bedded down or grazing near the water. Apparently Brissom hadn't troubled to run them too far up into the brush. Jess counted twenty cows and fifteen calves.

The men ground-tied their horses in the brush. McClaren made himself comfortable for the wait, melting into the deep shadows. He kept his Winchester in his hands.

Time passed slowly. Curly seemed inclined to conversation, but Jess managed to squelch him. The night grew sharp with chill. At this altitude a summer night felt like late fall. The air was scented with piñon and pine resin and the fresh breath of the trickling stream below. From time to time Jess rubbed his hands together to keep them from stiffening. Wind moved uneasily through the trees on the steep hillsides, masking other sounds.

Once Jess tensed for action when brush crackled nearby, until he realized that it was only Red moving around, shifting his position to one further downcanyon.

The wind stilled for a brief moment. Jess heard the scrape of a horseshoe on gravel from somewhere below and a low murmur of men's voices, lost in the next gust of wind sweeping over the ridges.

Jess's gray flung up her head. Immediately Jess was at her side, fingers over her nostrils, a quieting hand on her neck.

The three men waited tensely in the dark. The moon had set. It was impossible to see what went on below.

Still, Jess knew when the riders, at least two from the sounds, spooked the cattle to their feet and began to urge them downcanyon.

The three watchers had agreed not to challenge the thieves, but to try and follow them from a position too far back to be heard or seen. McClaren hoped they might learn something from the raiders' destination.

But fate was not on their side, this night. Warner's horse let out a shrill cry into the night, and it was more than enough to alert the rustlers to their presence.

McClaren, realizing even before the first shot whined from below that there would be no hope now of following their original plan, leaped into the saddle and sent the gray mare plunging down the hillside.

He had to trust to the mare's surefootedness, for he could see little or nothing of the ground in the darkness. He raised the rifle and fired one-handedly in the general direction of the rustlers. The slug passed close enough to somebody to startle him into a panicky yell.

There was gunfire from behind Jess. He bent low and hoped Red and Curly realized he was in their line of fire.

McClaren had cause to bless the gray's surefootedness as the rangy mare scrambled down and over the scattered rocks, humps of grass and weeds, the fallen tree trunks. She managed to reach the trail below without more than a slight stumble.

Jess heard the thud of hooves behind. The other men were mounted and following. He could see a bunched mass ahead of him. He fired into the thick of it.

Cattle scattered like deer off the trail, their heavy bodies crashing into the brush. Jess guessed the horsemen wouldn't risk riding blindly up the steep slopes, but would stick to the one trail. He kept the gray at a gallop.

He could hear a horse close ahead now. He spurred the mare to greater speed, gaining on the rider just in front of him, who was bent low over his saddle, whipping his cowpony hard.

Again Jess steadied the rifle, pulled the trigger. The man ahead cried out hoarsely, but did not fall, nor did his horse's pace falter.

Jess was gaining on the rustler fast. The rider straightened in his saddle, turning. Jess had a glimpse of a very tall, bulky figure. He sensed rather than saw the pistol in the man's hand, and bent over his mount's neck as the thief fired, but an instant too late. The bullet slammed into McClaren's body, the force of it almost lifting him out of the saddle.

"Pete? *Que pasa?*" someone shouted.

Jess managed to stay on the mare, but to no avail. The rustler's next shot, from only yards away, caught the gray in the chest. She went down like a child's jointed wooden toy. McClaren was flung away from the trail. Something connected with his skull, and he knew nothing more.

He woke to pain in his head that throbbed with an agonizing cadence, and a stinging pain in his right side. Groggily he opened his eyes, unable to focus. Slowly he was aware that he lay upon a bed, his upper body bare.

A sharpened pang in his side roused him to full awareness. He flinched and turned his head to find Maggie Bourne bending over him. Manuela stood to one side, a basin in her hands.

Maggie glanced up and caught his eyes on her. Her expression was frowning. "Sorry. The carbolic stings," she murmured.

"What's happened?" McClaren asked, trying to still the aching swim of his head.

"You were shot," she said severely, and he felt like a kid caught snitching cookies. "The bullet went through. I don't think it hit anything vital. Red's gone to Tularosa to fetch Doc Potter. You lost some blood, and have a cut and a bump on your head."

Abruptly McClaren remembered the last moments before he fell. "The rustlers?"

Maggie shrugged. "They got away. Red thinks you winged one of them. They didn't get the cattle."

She turned her head. "Manuela, will you bring that hot soup now? I've got the bandage on as well as I can."

"*Sí.*" Manuela set the basin on a table. She smiled at Jess. "You will soon be well again, Señor McClaren. We will take very good care of you, *muy bueno*."

"Sorry to be so much trouble," Jess grunted, reaching left-handedly to touch his head.

Maggie dipped a cloth in cold water and wrung it out. "You must have hit a rock when you fell. Red said your mount went down so fast he had no time to pull up and his pony fell too."

"Was he hurt?" McClaren asked sharply.

She shook her head. "He and Curly found you ten or fifteen feet down the slope. They thought at first that you were dead." Her lips were sternly compressed.

McClaren realized that she must have been gotten out of bed and given no time to dress. Her coppery hair was loose, flowing down her back and over her shoulders. She wore a faded flannel wrapper over her white nightdress. At his glance she flushed angrily and pulled the tie of the robe tighter.

She was not exactly pretty, McClaren decided. Her face was too strong for mere prettiness, the cheekbones too evident, with shadows slanting under them, shadows that led subtly to her mouth. And that mouth seemed incapable of laughter, though it was tenderly shaped. Her dark eyes were beautiful, but too direct.

Here was a woman who would not know how to flirt, who would not pretend to any emotion she did not feel.

Manuela came in, carrying a tray. McClaren's mouth watered at the smell of coffee and food. He tried to sit up, and gasped at the sudden pain in head and side.

Impersonally Maggie helped him, her slender arm strong beneath his shoulder as Manuela heaped pillows to support him. Jess felt like cursing his helplessness. It was the first time that he could remember being tended like a baby, and he could see little to recommend it.

"Shall I help you eat?" Maggie asked.

"I can manage!"

There was instant withdrawal in her face. Avoiding his eyes, she gathered up bandages and the basin of bloodied water and left the room.

Manuela drew the sheet up over McClaren's torso, set the tray on his lap, and left him to his meal. The sun was just coming up, making the lamplight wan.

He was shakier than he would have thought possible, and was grateful that no one was in the room to observe the unsteady journey of spoon to mouth. In spite of discomfort and weakness, he felt ravenous, wishing the soup might have been steak.

After eating, he slid the tray to one side, worked his body carefully down in the bed, and abandoned himself to sleep.

When he was awakened by Warner's arrival with the doctor, he found that the day was more than three quarters gone, and with it some of his headache.

Doc Potter, a small man dressed in a wrinkled suit, his whiskers stained by chewing tobacco and his breath not innocent of whiskey, removed the dressing Maggie had applied that morning, his fingers brisk and ungentle.

Jess winced as the elderly physician probed at his side, mumbling unintelligibly under his breath. The doctor poured something that had been distilled amid the fires of hell upon the wound and rebandaged it. Jess wished fiercely that he dared request that Maggie tend to it instead. He closed his eyes, remembering the clean, healthy scent of her, leaning close, the gleam of her hair in the lamplight—

"You'll live, I don't doubt," pronounced the doctor. "Best stay in bed a few days, let that heal."

"I can't spare a few days. What do I owe you?"

"Miss Bourne assured me Mr. Whitley will pay."

Jess felt crankier than a range bull just yanked from a mud hole. "I pay my own bills! How much?"

The little man shrugged, asked for two dollars. Red Warner fetched the money from McClaren's saddlebag that lay over a chairback. As the doctor departed, Jess heaved himself upright in bed, ignoring the pain and weakness.

"Find my shirt, Red," he demanded.

Warner grinned. "You heard the doc. You got to stay corralled for a spell."

"Not my style. Give me my shirt!"

"Manuela took all your stuff to be washed. All you got to wear is the pants you got on."

Frustrated, McClaren lurched to his feet, holding on to the bedpost for a minute until he could navigate.

"Well then, I guess I'll go without."

The door opened and Maggie Bourne strode in, staring with astonishment at the swaying McClaren.

"Miss Bourne, don't you start in on me too," he warned. "I ain't about to get in that bed again. It must be about suppertime, and I intend to see about my horses before dark."

"Your horses are in better shape than you, by a long shot," commented a grinning Red. "And you are gonna shock all the ladies if you go running around half-naked."

Surprisingly, Maggie did not add her arguments to Red's. She studied McClaren for a long minute, then sighed. "I'll bring one of Joe Ed's shirts. If you fall on your face, it's your own doing."

"I want some hot water too." McClaren pushed his luck recklessly. She turned with a graceful swirl of skirts and went out.

"Godamighty, cowboy!" Warner hooted. "I think that lady likes you!"

* * *

Maggie supplied not only a shirt, but a pair of pants that were only a little short for McClaren's tall frame. Manuela brought a can of hot water, and both women left without comment.

Red, uninvited, stood by to lend a hand should the invalid be unable to manage his sketchy wash.

When he was clean and dressed, McClaren felt as tired as if he'd chased steers through the brush country all day, but pleased with himself. He had even managed one-handedly to get his boots on. Funny how helpless it made a man feel to be without his boots.

He insisted on visiting the corrals before supper. Warner casually trailed along. To tell the truth, Jess wasn't sorry to have him. For one thing, he wanted Red's version of last night's events.

"You get a look at any of them?" he asked the redhead.

"Not a peep. You was first on their tails, and when your horse went down, it threw mine all of a heap. By the time I got straightened out, they was long gone. You see anything?" He shot Jess a penetrating glance, seemed to wait tensely for the answer, but Jess had little to offer.

"Got a little look at one of them. A big man. One of his buddies yelled for Pete. Could have meant the one I saw."

Warner leaned on the corral, gazed at the horses within. "That could be any one of half a dozen fellers, or somebody not from these parts."

"They knew where to look for those cows. Likely they'd kept an eye on the water holes and picked the one where the most stock had gathered."

Red shrugged. "Wellsir, even a stranger might do that. It ain't that hard to find the springs in these canyons."

"We need to ride more, check every main watering place, see if anyone's been prowling around. We can get a better idea of where most of the cows are staying, and where trouble might come next."

"You won't be riding for a time," Warner said. "Me and the boys will handle it until you heal up."

Manuela rang the bell on the porch, signaling supper. Jess felt somewhat better for the walk in the fresh air, and the good hot food gave him new strength.

Maggie was at the table tonight. Apparently Mrs. Whitley ate in her room.

Once, Jess glanced up from his plate to find Maggie watching him with an unreadable look. He smiled. She ignored it, jerking her eyes to Joey, warning him not to play with his food. Odd, because the boy was shoveling the grub in steadily.

"Yes ma'am," Joey mumbled with full mouth, undisturbed.

After supper, McClaren headed for the back door, but was stopped by Manuela and a whispered message. Mrs. Whitley wished to speak privately with him. Curious, Jess followed the cook's directions to the front parlor.

Here, amid little-used horsehide furniture, the lace curtains and gewgaws on little stands and corner shelves, McClaren found the rancher's wife. She was seated by a window. In the late evening light, her hair gleamed softly, and her face seemed younger. She was still a pretty woman. It was obvious she had taken pains to hang on to the beauty of her youth.

Judging from the reception she'd given him the first day, McClaren assumed Mrs. Whitley had no use for him. He was startled by her cordial smile as he halted just inside the doorway, hat in hand.

"Please do come in and sit down, Mr. McClaren," she murmured. "You must be feeling your wound, and I wouldn't want to tire you."

Jess sat on the edge of the uncomfortable sofa. She was right, he was feeling the wound, and it made his supper roil uncomfortably in his stomach. He hoped she would say whatever she had to say in a hurry. "What can I do for you, Mrs. Whitley?"

She smiled charmingly. "I am told that you and the other men engaged in a dangerous gunfight last night."

McClaren considered this remark, one eyebrow raised. "I reckon any gunfight is dangerous, ma'am."

"But you were shot, and could well have been killed!" She clasped her small white hands to her breast. "Oh, I will never understand you men! Why must you put yourselves in harm's way so recklessly? We have already had one of our riders killed. I would not like to see that happen to you, Mr. McClaren, indeed I would not."

"Nor would I." McClaren wished she would get to the point. His head was beginning to add its complaints to the pain in his side, and he was ready to get back to the bed he had so stubbornly quit earlier.

The blond woman rose and came to settle gracefully on the couch at his side. "I can see you're a fine young man, Jess." She touched his hand, the softness of her fingers resting for a long moment on his. "But this is not your fight."

"I've promised to help your husband."

"When you made that promise, you couldn't have known that you were risking your life. No one would blame you if you reconsidered."

Her hand was still on his, and her eyes held a promise he couldn't quite believe. Anna Whitley's tongue parted her lips, the tip moist and pink.

Jess stood quickly, wincing at the twinge of his bandaged side. "You needn't fret on my account, Mrs. Whitley. You have your husband to worry about. And I can take care of myself."

She drew back sharply, as if he had slapped her.

"Excuse me, ma'am," Jess muttered, and hurried from the room.

He strode along the hall, but stopped as his side sent a knife-sharp pain across his body. He drew a slow breath, head down, eyes shut.

"Does it hurt awful bad?"

Joey stood before him, eyes round with concern. Jess straightened, with an effort.

"Only a little bit, son. I guess I'll go to my room."

Joey grabbed Jess's hand. "I'll pull off your boots. I always help Grandpa."

So the little boy saved Jess the misery of bending and wrenching at his boots. He also helped McClaren out of his shirt and turned back the bedclothes.

"You want I should light the lamp?" Joey asked.

"No thanks, Joey. Guess I'll get some shuteye."

"You ain't afraid of the dark?"

McClaren grinned. "Only now and then. How about you?"

"No sir." Joey sat down on the bed, causing McClaren's wound to twinge again. "Can I stay with you until you go to sleep?" he asked.

"Sure, if you want."

"I'll be quiet, like when I sit with Grandpa. Maggie says a man's gotta know when to keep still. Sometimes Grandpa don't even know I'm there."

"Okay, son," Jess mumbled, already half-asleep.

He dozed, and dreamed of Maggie Bourne leaning over him, her face softer than he had ever seen it, filled with worry.

A small sound woke him. He opened his eyes to see Joey being quietly urged from the room by his mother.

Chapter Six

"Miss Bourne?" Jess murmured.

She hesitated, then touched her son's hair. "Go to bed, Joey. I'll come in a few minutes to tuck you in." She came back to Jess's bed.

"Yes, Mr. McClaren. Do you need something?" Her voice was clear and cool as a mountain stream. And just as indifferent.

He could not clearly see her face in the dark room, but he knew that her expression would be grave and forbidding.

Impulsively he reached for her hand, held the slender fingers. After a startled moment, she pulled free. "Did you want something?" she repeated icily.

Want something? Yes. Maybe he would never have known it if he had not wakened to find her in the room, warming it in spite of the distance she held between them. He knew if he tried to tell her of his confused emotions, the new raw longings that were growing in his mind and body, she would immediately put a wall between them. He had known her too brief a time. She would not understand how, in some lost, secret place deep within his mind, he had searched for Maggie Bourne all his life.

He sighed and made his words ordinary. "That's a fine boy you got," he said.

"Thank you, Mr. McClaren."

"Good night, Maggie."

She stared at him, puzzlement in those wide dark eyes. "Good night, Mr. McClaren," she said at last, and left him, closing the door firmly behind her.

McClaren's next three days were those of a semi-invalid. The cut on his head proved negligible. But the bullet wound was painful, stiff, and generally a damned nuisance.

Jess did not allow this to keep him idle, using the time to help José mend one of the corrals. The second afternoon he felt well enough to attempt to ride, and caught Capitan up from the horse pasture.

The big bay was lively after his rest and good feed. McClaren eased the heavy stock saddle upon the sleek back. Carefully he boosted himself into the saddle. The bay danced eagerly under him, and Jess let the horse move out.

But even the stallion's silken-footed gait was a little too much. McClaren stood it for fifteen minutes, then unsaddled the stud.

José's intelligent eyes took in the situation, but he was tactful enough not to comment. Very casually he lifted the saddle and other gear and returned it to the barn before McClaren could do it.

Jess sat on the edge of a rock water tank, trying not to let on how badly he needed to rest. He nodded his thanks as José came back, then looked at the boy thoughtfully.

"José, I need to get into town. Could you drive me down in the buckboard?"

José nodded. "Oh, yes, but not today. I think maybe *mañana* is better."

Jess grinned wryly. "I expect you're right, son. Let's get back to the fence."

José protested, but McClaren insisted on helping, his face still white under the tan. He was lifting oak poles into place when Joey came running to the stables, shouting for him.

"Jess, my grandpa wants to talk to you."

McClaren wiped sweat from his face and went up to the house with the little boy skipping at his side. They went in at the kitchen door. Maggie was peeling potatoes. She looked up as he came in and frowned. "Mr. McClaren, you shouldn't be working so hard just yet. Your wound isn't properly healed."

"Cain't seem to stay put, Maggie." He grinned at her, his frank gaze daring her to smile back. Hastily she dropped her gaze to the vegetables in front of her.

"Joe Ed wants to talk with you," she said.

"How is he today?"

Her expression lightened magically. "Much better. He's able to be up for a few minutes a day. Joe Ed hates being bedridden. I suppose he has that in common with you, Mr. McClaren."

"You can tell the world! I'll go see what he wants."

Jess found Whitley propped upright on pillows, looking mean enough to fight mountain lions bare-fisted.

"Come in here, son!" he growled. "Set down. How come I ain't seen you for two days?"

McClaren could hardly admit he'd stayed away deliberately until the effects of his wounds were not so apparent. It would have done the old man no good to let him know about the gunfight.

"Sorry, sir. Guess I just got busy."

"I hear you got yourself shot at," accused Whitley.

"Where'd you hear that?" Jess was amazed that anyone could have slipped the word past Maggie.

"Joey."

Jess sighed. "Uh-huh."

"Wellsir, I mean to hear about it. Spit it out."

"Ain't nothin' to fret about, sir. The boys and I had a little difference of opinion with some fellers over in Evening Star Canyon. It was their opinion they could borrow a few head of cows. We disagreed."

Joe Ed's mouth pursed and he gazed at McClaren from under heavy white brows. "Find out who they was?"

Jess grinned. "They didn't introduce themselves, but then I guess there wasn't time for a lot of socializing. I got a little look at one of 'em. Big man, wide as a barn door."

Jess rubbed a hand along his jaw. "If I'd ducked sooner when he threw down on me, I might have been able to stay on their trail long enough to find out something. But I went down and brought Red down with me. I lost a good mare of yours, Mr. Whitley. I'm sure sorry, and I'll pay you for her."

The elderly man seemed so affronted by this suggestion that Jess quickly dropped it. Whitley fixed his eyes on Jess's face.

"You sorry you got into this, boy?"

"I owe you, Mr. Whitley. My pa thought a lot of you."

"That ain't what I asked you."

Jess shook his head. "I'm not sorry."

Whitley's age-spotted big hand pulled impatiently at the edge of the bright pieced quilt. "I wouldn't never ask for help if I could git outta this bed and do the job my own self." Whitley's voice was frustrated.

"At one time I could have. I fought Apaches and some good Mexican folk down to Tularosa who didn't like us up in the hills using the water. I've outfoxed cow thieves aplenty, and catamounts and coyotes to hold this here spread. I want it to go to Maggie when I'm gone. But someone shore is aimin' to take it away from me. If I wasn't as wobble-legged as a sick calf, I'd hunt down whoever is runnin' off my cows and bushwhacking my riders. I'd see they hang if I had to put the noose around their mangy necks with these two hands!" He held them up, clenched into massive fists that shook with weakness and fury.

Jess nodded. "I'd feel the same, Mr. Whitley."

"I hate asking another man to do my snake stomping for me. The law in this territory cain't seem to do much with all the lowlifes that have moved in of late. An' it ain't just newcomers that you daren't turn your back on.

"There's cowmen been in these parts thirty year who ain't above spooking a neighbor's stock across the

Rio Grande. Mostly they prey on the big ranches. Chisum, down on the South Springs, has lost a lot of cows. Reckon most cowmen has lost a few. I ain't never used another man's beef on the sly, an' I never will. I don't mind losing a few head o' beef now and then to a man who cain't feed his children. But somebody has been trying to clean me out. I won't tolerate that."

"You think this somebody is aiming to buy your spread cheap?"

Whitley nodded. "Or maybe just to take over, after me and mine are out of the way. There was that old man they called Frenchy. Settled in Dog Canyon on good water some years back, right under the noses of the Apache. Every man in the territory was betting he'd lose his scalp. But it weren't Indians got him. That much is known, though no one ain't saying no names, and the law never was much interested in takin' no one in for it."

He sighed and shifted in the bed. "Then they was the Nesmith murder—in eighty-two I believe it was. Nesmith testified to a certain cow thief's deeds in a court of law. The thief, who it is said had eight hundred thousand dollars and a good ranch, got off with a fifteen-hundred-dollar fine. The Nesmiths and their little girl was found chewed by varmints and entertaining the buzzards in the White Sands."

He looked at McClaren. "It's dangerous times, son, worse because of the drought. There's men would kill for a good supply of water. Maybe that's what they're after here, whoever they are. I hope you can find out. I got to provide for my girl Maggie and Joey."

"A man wants to put something aside for his family."

As if he sensed criticism, Whitley said, "There's five thousand dollars in a Las Cruces bank for my wife. She is provided for. But the ranch is to go to Maggie and little Joey. If we can hold it fer 'em."

"I'll do all I can, Mr. Whitley."

Whitley's eyes wandered to the window and the summer landscape outside. He seemed to stray from the subject.

"My Maggie's a good girl. She's got backbone. She can ride better'n any man on the place and she knows as much about cows as I do. You'll hear talk about Maggie, if you ain't already, which ain't likely, her with a little son and no wedding ring. Don't you believe none of it! The only thing she ever done wrong was to love too fierce and trust too much. She's got a big heart. You maybe cain't see that. Since her trouble, an' them town women drawing their skirts aside and putting their snotty noses in the air when Maggie passes, she's—harder. She's put her sweetness and gentleness away. She had to, McClaren, that or break.

"But deep down, my Maggie's warm and loving. She tends me hand and foot and never a complaint from her."

"She's a fine woman," Jess agreed readily.

Whitley fixed him with keen old eyes. "You don't hold it against her none, her having the boy?"

"It's none of my business."

Whitley seemed about to say more, but at that moment Mrs. Whitley bustled into the room with a swish of silken skirts. Her striped blue and white dress was lace trimmed, more appropriate for city streets than a ranch house.

"Why Jess!" She smiled brightly. "How good of you to sit with Mr. Whitley." She touched Joe Ed's face. "You mustn't strain yourself, my dear," she chided. "Don't you think you have visited long enough?"

Hastily McClaren stood. Whitley moved his face impatiently away from his wife's fingers.

"I'd better go." Jess strode toward the door.

"Oh, Mr. McClaren, may I have a word with you?" Mrs. Whitley called after him in a girlish voice.

McClaren turned. Beyond her he saw that Whitley's face had gone rigid as seamed granite. Whitley is nobody's fool, Jess thought.

"Sorry, ma'am," Jess answered coolly. "I left a job half-finished out at the corrals."

"Perhaps later, then," she purred, eyes bright in the white, pampered skin of her face, her smile coaxing.

Jess mumbled something and left the room, wondering why a man like Joe Ed had tied up with a woman like Anna Whitley.

She wasn't the first of her type that McClaren had

encountered. Most of them were found on the side of the towns where no decent woman would set foot. Pretty in youth, sought after by men, they never seemed to realize the loss of that prettiness as age approached. They were like bloodsucking horseflies, always seeking a new host.

No wonder Joe Ed's deepest regard was reserved for Maggie and the boy.

Early next morning José brought the ranch buggy around to the kitchen door. McClaren was just finishing breakfast. With a sudden thought he glanced at Maggie, who was clearing the table. "I'm going to Tularosa today, Maggie. Maybe you'd like to come along."

Surprised, she hesitated. "Why—I—"

"Me too!" Joey demanded.

Jess shook his head. "Not this time, son. I'll bring you some penny candy."

Joey had started to frown mutinously but brightened at the promise.

"How about it, Maggie?" Jess persisted.

"Well, I would like to shop for a few things. I promised Manuela cloth to make a dress, and we need meal and coffee."

"Good." McClaren rose. "I'll wait for you outside."

"I won't be a minute." She cast off her apron, revealing the trim lines of a flowered cotton dress that was a pleasing combination of blues and greens.

Jess stepped out to tell José that he wouldn't be needing him after all, that Miss Bourne was going. The young man grinned.

"Ah, I am not half so pretty as Miss Maggie!"

McClaren stepped into the buggy as Maggie hurried out, pushing a list of needed items into her purse. She had taken time to twist the long braid down her back into a knot at the nape of her neck. But haste had left her usually severe hairstyle somewhat loosened. Curling strands escaped about her temples. Carrying a white knitted shawl, she ran down the steps as lightly as a child. Forlorn again, Joey stood waving.

McClaren reached his left hand to help Maggie into

the buggy, then he set the horse trotting on the wagon road downcanyon. Maggie's face was pink from her haste. She looked prettier than Jess had ever seen her.

At the bend in the road he looked back at the ranch house. The early sun tinted its adobe sides rosy. Amid its cottonwoods and evergreens, it might have stood there secure against the outer world forever.

I like it here, McClaren thought. I like the mountains and the way the Tularosa Basin stretches out to the Sands and the San Andres. It gives a man's eyes something to enjoy. And, he added to himself, I like having this girl beside me.

Maggie looked back too, self-reproachful. "I shouldn't have left Manuela with all the work. She was going to bake today, and I intended—"

"Manuela won't mind," McClaren said.

"Still, I don't like to burden her unnecessarily—"

"Shut up, Maggie Bourne, and enjoy yourself, or I'll set you out to walk back," McClaren drawled, poker-faced.

Startled, she glanced at him, saw he was teasing. Her lips curved in a faint, reluctant smile. It changed the lines of her face. McClaren had his first glimpse of the carefree girl she had once been. And he wouldn't have traded that moment for a hatful of railroad shares.

The morning air was sweet and cool, but when they reached the desert, it would be another scorching day, McClaren knew, studying the hard blue of the cloudless sky.

When the silence stretched out too long, Jess coaxed from Maggie the names of springs and meadows they passed. Her voice became animated, happy.

"You love this country, don't you?" he asked.

She seemed surprised at the question. "Why, I grew up here, Mr. McClaren. I'm afraid I shall never love another place as well."

"Maybe you'll never have to get used to another place."

Her fine brows drew together. "No, it's only a matter of time until I'll have to leave J-bar-W. Joe Ed is never going to be well again. I'm here only on his sufferance. When he is—when he's gone, then I must leave here."

McClaren realized that she had no idea of Whitley's plan to leave the ranch to her. "What makes you so sure of that?" he asked.

She hesitated, then said steadily, "Because then Daniel Whitley will be coming back. And Anna and I are not—friends."

McClaren grunted. "Doubt if Mrs. Whitley has any friends." He risked a question. "Why couldn't you stay on J-bar-W even if Whitley's son comes home?"

She was silent so long that he glanced at her and could scarcely believe the change in her expression. She looked older, strained, and when she met his eyes it was with a cold—yet stricken—purpose. McClaren was put in mind of a child made to confess to a painful truth.

He saw her swallow. "How much do you know about Daniel Whitley?" she asked.

He evaded. "No one seems to want to talk about the man."

"When I was sixteen," she said in a flat voice, her eyes fixed on the buggy horse, "I was—in love with Daniel. He was several years older than I, and very handsome. Daniel was always coaxing me to—be alone with him."

With a sense of shame, Jess wondered if he should tell her that he already knew what she was about to tell him. Something warned him it was best to let her talk about it. Maybe she needed to spit out that old pain.

"Nothing very strange about that," he said quietly.

He felt her swift glance. "Joe Ed had warned me to be careful around the men, even Daniel. I guess he knew—" She stopped, drew an unsteady breath.

"I knew Joe Ed was right, and I refused Daniel. He was furious, and left home for days. When he came back, he told me about girls in the cantinas who weren't so stubborn. I was afraid he would leave and never come back, but I couldn't go against Joe Ed. Finally, Daniel asked me to marry him. I"—her voice faltered—"I was so happy. I told Joe Ed and Mrs. Whitley.

Anna had a fit, refused to hear of our marrying. She said her son could do a lot better than a—a penniless orphan. Joe Ed spoke sharply to her for that, but he was no more pleased with the idea than she was. He said I was too young, that I needed to meet other young men, not rush into marriage.

"I promised Joe Ed I would wait a few months. But—I loved Danny. I was a fool where he was concerned. When he came to my room one night and said he had arranged for us to be married in La Luz, I went with him."

McClaren looked at her, concealing surprise. This was the first mention he'd heard of a marriage between Maggie and Daniel Whitley.

"Then—" he began.

"Let me finish," she said tensely. "He took me to a boardinghouse in La Luz and slipped me up the stairs to a room. I asked him why we had to make a secret of it, and he claimed he was afraid Joe Ed would come after us. Daniel called his father a stubborn, opinionated old fool. I didn't believe that, and I didn't like hearing it. But I loved Daniel, and I was ready to do whatever he said was best."

She pounded her knee with a clenched fist. "I was a fool, Mr. McClaren. What a stupid fool I was!"

"You got no call to feel that way," Jess broke in. "You're not the first girl to be fooled, nor the last. I knew a girl, real pretty girl, brought up right. She fell in love with a good-lookin' drifter who left her in the family way. She killed herself."

"Maybe that's what I should have done." Maggie's eyes were wide and anguished.

"That's fool talk!" Jess gave her a stern look. "Surely you aren't ashamed of that little boy of yours. He'll be a fine man someday."

She bit her lip. "No. No, I shouldn't have said that. It was just—remembering."

"It's all water under the bridge. Try to put it out of your mind."

She shook her head. "I can't. And I want you to know the truth of it."

After a moment to control her emotion, she continued. "Daniel took me to the room. There was an old man there, shabby, dressed in black. He was—I realized later—more than half-drunk. But—he married us."

Jess turned to her. "Then you are—"

She shook her head, a brief, sharp negation. "It was all a lie. Danny knew I wouldn't give in to him without marriage. Joe Ed had taught me too carefully. Danny staged it all, and I was completely fooled.

"I wanted to go home right away," she remembered, face drawn. "I wanted to tell Joe Ed we were married. I knew he wouldn't object, now that it was done. But Daniel gave the preacher money and hustled him out. Then he locked the door and put the key where I couldn't get it."

"Maggie, don't—" McClaren protested, but she continued woodenly, as if she had not heard him.

"It—wasn't like I had thought it would be," she whispered. "I was hating Daniel long before that awful night was over. He hurt me, and when I cried, he beat me. When I woke in the morning, he was dressed and ready to leave. I asked him where he was going. He laughed, said it was none of my business."

She took a deep, quivering breath to steady herself, and McClaren felt a murderous rage against the man who had brutalized Maggie Bourne.

Her voice was ragged. "Daniel said that it was all a joke. The man who'd married us was just an old bum he'd found in a saloon. He said it served me right for being so high and mighty with him, when I was nothing and nobody—"

McClaren laid his hand over her clenched fists, feeling the unbearable tension in them. She jerked her hands away.

"What did you do then?" he asked, wishing that he had Daniel Whitley's neck in his hands at that moment.

"He left. I got up, dressed. I felt very cold, and I was shaking. I couldn't think clearly. I couldn't believe it had happened, and all I wanted was to go home.

"I crept down the stairs. A woman was on her way up, and she looked at me as if I were a piece of dirt. No wonder. My face was bruised, and my hair was down—" She shuddered, and her shoulders bent as if weighed down.

"I ran out into the streets. I had no horse, no money to hire one. People stared at me as I ran along the road, but I couldn't think of asking any of them to help me."

"You couldn't have walked all the way home!"

"I tried, straight out across the desert. I had no water. I hoped I would die, but Joe Ed found me in the afternoon, and took me home. Then he went looking for his son. I heard that he forbade Daniel ever to set foot on the ranch again. How Anna hated me, after that! Daniel meant more to her than anything else in her life, and she was convinced that I had driven him out of his home."

"Has Daniel ever come back?"

She sighed. "No. But he will when his father is gone. I never want to lay eyes on him again."

She fell silent. Clucking to the horse, McClaren turned the buggy into the basin road. He longed to comfort Maggie, but she was stiffly withdrawn from him now. The wrong that had been done this woman was long in the past, but she was still hating, and the hatred seemed to spill over on every man, except Joe Ed.

Jess wondered why she had told him her story. Maybe it had been souring inside her for so long that she had to get it all out, to the first stranger who would listen.

But if she had been seeking someone uninvolved and indifferent, she had come to the wrong man.

Chapter Seven

It was almost noon when they came into Tularosa. McClaren looked about him with interest.

It was a pleasant village, especially on a hot summer day. The streets were lined with cottonwood trees arching their shady tops overhead. The buildings were mostly of adobe, large, flat-roofed and thick-walled, built around patios in the Mexican style. In the square around the church there was a vineyard, and even fruit trees. Water flowed, if sluggishly, in some of the *acequias,* water drawn from the Tularosa River. In a good year there would be ample irrigation water for the gardens and the fruit, and it would seem an oasis to all who came here.

Maggie asked to stop at a general store. McClaren hitched the horse and went in with her.

A thin, distinguished-looking Mexican came forward and spoke courteously to Maggie, giving her a courtly little bow. But two women who were fingering the dress goods pointedly turned their heads without greeting and moved away as Maggie passed nearby.

With an instinct to protect her, McClaren joined her by a counter lined with bolts of cloth. Immediately the women turned to examine him with avid curiosity, and one whispered behind her gloved hand to the other.

McClaren felt his neck redden and reflected that respectable women could be mean as hell.

Maggie glanced sidewise at him, and her look was bitter. "It's quite all right, Mr. McClaren," she said very clearly. "I'm used to it by now. I should warn you that if you stay too near me, your name will be linked with mine within a week on every ranch and in every *placita* in Lincoln County."

He heard shocked gasps from the other ladies. "Well I never!" said one, her bonnet feather trembling with indignation.

Jess grinned. "Oh, I reckon I can bear up under it," he murmured under his breath, his eyes steadily upon her wide brown ones. It did something very pleasant to him to see her slim face warm with sudden color.

However, he had no wish to embarrass her, so he moved away as if he had merely asked her a question of a business nature, as a hired hand might be expected to.

Jess bought two pairs of Levi's pants and a couple of plain gray flannel shirts, and a bag of striped candy for Joey. After paying his bill, he asked the way to a barber, told Maggie he would pick her up in an hour, and strode out of the store.

He had noticed that barbers were frequently incurable gossips, and a trim sure wouldn't do his hair and beard any harm.

He was disappointed in his barber, however. Jess's casual remarks about the rustlers on the J-bar-W and careful questions as to strangers in town drew no helpful information. The greatest benefit was to his sore side—the barber chair was comfortable.

Jess looked a different and more respectable citizen when he left the shop, with his beard shaped neatly to his strong jaw and hair clipped to his collar.

There was time to try one more thing. He found the biggest cantina in town. It was dim and cool inside and almost empty at this time of day, but there were two elderly men playing poker at a table in back and one nursing a drink at the bar.

McClaren asked for beer. When the bartender brought it, Jess raised his voice to be audible to everyone in the place. "Say, mister, I'm looking for a feller. His friends call him Pete. Great big man, built like a bull."

The dapper bartender paused in the act of wiping up a spill. "You the law?"

Jess grinned. "Do I look like it?"

The barkeep eyed him narrowly. "I think you look like a Texan. You could be a Ranger. Or maybe not.

It don't matter. I don't know this man you're askin' about."

McClaren shrugged. "Well, it ain't that important. I got a message for him. Man from San Antone described him to me, said he hangs out in these parts."

One of the elderly poker players abruptly left the cantina. Jess had a feeling the departure had something to do with him. He finished his drink and walked out, ambling along the street toward the buggy, his eyes alert for trouble. That old man had left the bar for some reason, and it could have been to alert somebody. A warning buzzed like a rattler at the back of Jess's brain.

A faint whistle from an alley made Jess whirl toward the sound, sharply reminded of his healing side. His gun was out before he was fully turned, but he let it slide back into the holster when he saw the gray-haired poker player beckoning him from a door in the side of a store building.

McClaren glanced about him. Apparently no one was paying any attention. He moved at an indifferent pace into the littered alley.

"Mister, I heard what you said in there," hurriedly mumbled the skinny oldster, who had the look of a stove-up cowpoke. "What you want with this feller, Pete?"

"Like I said. I got a message for him."

"Mister, it looks to me like you got serious business on yore mind. You from Texas?"

McClaren nodded. The old man pursed his mouth and pulled at a tobacco-stained, drooping mustache.

"I grew up down in the Llano Estacado myself. Learned young to tell a honest man from a skunk, an' that's why I'm alive today. I hope you'll take this advice kindly. You had better be mighty careful where at you go askin' a lot of questions."

"You know something about this Pete?"

The old cowboy blinked pale eyes that had grown dim from studying distances. "Reckon you didn't hear what I said."

McClaren took a chance. "The man I'm lookin' for put a bullet through my side a few days ago when I caught him inviting the boss's cows for a moonlight stroll. My boss is a good man. He's old and he's sick. He hasn't got a lot more years, and he wants to leave his family what he has fought for all his life. I aim to help him. Whatever it takes."

There was instant sympathy in the older man's face. "Who is this feller you're a-workin' fer?"

"Joe Ed Whitley of J-bar-W."

The man's mouth fell open, revealing toothless gums. "You work for Joe Ed? Why, him and me run together years ago, when he first settled hereabouts. I ain't seen ol' Joe Ed for a coon's age. I had me a little cow ranch over to Eagle Creek, east side o' the Sacramentos. But I fooled around an' lost it, and then I drifted up into Montana, worked fer first one ranch an' then another until I got too damned old. When I come back here, I thought about looking up Joe Ed Whitley, fer I know he's a honest man, an' I thought he might give me a job. But I can't ride much no more, and I didn't want nobody thinking I was beggin' a handout."

Jess nodded, knowing this man's pride as he knew his own. "If you'd like to work for Joe Ed, I'll put in a word for you," he offered. "Mr. Whitley would be proud to have an old friend on J-bar-W."

"You'd do that fer me, son?"

"It's a small thing, mister."

"Well, now." The older man grinned toothlessly. "Well, fry my bacon, if this ain't my lucky day! Mister, I owe you one, so I'll give you a hint, though I might not be doing you no real favor atall. This Pete you are after sounds like Pete Gabaldon. He's big, mean as they come, and a dead shot. He got hisself hurt a few nights ago, the talk is." He glanced around and lowered his voice. "I heard he's hiding out over in the Jornada until he gets over what ails him. You wouldn't know nothing about ol' Pete's complaint, would you, son?"

McClaren grinned and ran a big hand over his newly trimmed beard. "I might. Thought I winged him before he got me, but I couldn't tell it did him a whole lot of harm."

"You dead set on finding him?"

"He's the only link I know to whoever is trying to make trouble for Mr. Whitley. I need to learn who he works for, or if he's behind the rustling himself."

The old man shook his head. "Bound to be someone else doing the thinking for Gabaldon. He ain't too bright. But he is a bad man, son, and he's got a way of confusin' his back trail that's slicker than a mangy coyote. It don't hurt his feelin's none to bushwhack somebody, I hear."

"Thanks for the hint." Jess nodded. "What is your name? I'll tell Joe Ed to expect you. You got a horse?"

Instant temper mottled the creased skin. "Well, of course I got a horse! I ain't that far gone I'd sell my pony and saddle. You tell Joe Ed that George Owens will be dropping by to chew over old times."

"There'll be a job waiting for you."

Mr. Owens nodded, with dignity. He might be down and out, Jess thought, but he was cut from solid cloth.

Jess was early getting back to the general store. He carried out Maggie's bundles. "Where can we buy a good dinner?" he asked her.

Maggie blinked. "Why, the hotel, I suppose. But"—she had that familiar little frown between her fine brows—"you don't mean to take me with you, surely."

He smiled. "Why no, ma'am. I reckoned you would wait for me in the buggy while I enjoy my meal."

Looking flustered and nervous, she gave him directions. Jess sent the horse at a brisk trot along the street and around the corner. As he helped her down, he was conscious that her hand trembled. Once more he inwardly cursed the pious women of this community who had made Maggie afraid of so simple a thing as walking into a hotel.

With a kind of defiant pride, Jess escorted her into the hotel dining room, held her chair, and ordered a meal for them both. He wondered if she had ever experienced this simple pleasure. She seemed to be losing her nervousness, and a kind of shy delight showed through the tough veneer of her reserve. It made her face youthful and soft.

McClaren caught the sidelong looks of other diners who apparently recognized Maggie Bourne. He quelled them with his own icy-gray gaze and tried to keep Maggie from being too much aware of the interest of the other folks. Apparently he was successful, for she ate her meal with enjoyment.

The ride back to the ranch was spent in quiet conversation. Maggie showed a courteous interest in Jess's parents, his boyhood, anything he cared to tell. Yet she never relaxed entirely. The barriers were still firmly in place.

"Where do you intend to settle?" she asked.

He realized that he had not thought that far ahead for days. When he had left Texas, the wanderlust had been strong in him. He had wanted to ride every mile between him and the sunset.

That longing was gone now, and he felt an unexpected sense of loss at the thought of leaving J-bar-W. He had not far to look for the reason. He told himself that here was something he had better weed out of his thinking, as Maggie dragged weeds from her small, cherished garden.

After all, he had nothing to offer a woman. And if he was successful in helping Joe Ed Whitley, Maggie would one day be the holder of modest wealth. The ranch would be worth more and more as the importance of good grazing land and permanent sources of water was realized by the settlers of this turbulent land. Maggie would have ample money. There would be men in plenty willing to overlook the fact that she had a son born out of wedlock, in view of her many profitable acres.

But Jess McClaren would not be among that group. It might be years before he could match what Maggie would be able to call her own. Until then, he would stand back from her, no matter how the sweetness of her presence made his soul ache—

She repeated her question, seeming puzzled at his long silence. He shoved back his longing to tell her that he wanted nothing so much as to stay and stand between her and anyone or anything that might bring hurt to her. Carefully lighthearted, he declared that he never intended to stay long enough in one place to let it become important to him.

"Ol' Capitan and me, reckon we'll just chase the end of the rainbow." he said, and would not let himself look at her to see if she approved of his statement.

Jess slept restlessly that night. Dreams disturbed him, dreams that involved Maggie Bourne. Come morning, he resolutely put them out of his mind and made his plans for the day. He found with satisfaction that the trip to Tularosa hadn't tired him much. His side was less sore this morning.

He was eager to act on his new information about Pete Gabaldon, but knew he'd best wait until he was better healed before tackling the rustler. If he could find him at all. From what he'd heard the Jornada was big, and singularly inhospitable. Men there were not eager to see a stranger's face. Questions would be about as welcome as the drought.

He fretted at the delay. Well, at least he could keep his promise to George Owens. Directly after breakfast he went in to see Joe Ed.

The rancher was sitting up in a chair, looking pleased with life and polishing off steak and eggs. He was tickled to hear that his old friend Owens would be coming.

"He's down on his luck, a little," Jess told Whitley. "He needs a job, but he's mighty proud. I told him you could use another hand."

"Well now, you did right, son. But he don't need to work. There's plenty room in the bunkhouse and plenty room at my table."

McClaren shook his head. "I don't think he wants a free ride, Mr. Whitley. He'll bow up his neck if you suggest that. But if he feels like you need him here, he'll be proud to sign on the crew."

Joe Ed looked thoughtful. "You got sense, young man."

"Appreciate you sayin' so," Jess said, and stood to go.

"Sit down, sit down, son." Whitley gestured impatiently. "There's something on my mind. But first, shut the door. Women got ears like a damn fox."

Jess did as he was asked, then seated himself near the older man.

"McClaren, what do you think of Maggie?" Whitley asked abruptly. "She's ain't a bad-looking girl, is she? And she can be trusted, not like some."

Puzzled, Jess studied Joe Ed, wondering how he ought to answer.

"Now, don't feed me no sugar water, son. Tell me straight."

McClaren rubbed his beard. "Wellsir, I think Maggie's all you say and more. You brought her up real fine."

"It don't bother you none that she has a woodscolt?"

"I think I told you before, I don't consider that my business."

Whitley coughed, regained his breath. "I'm—I'm asking you to make it your business, Jess."

Not getting the old man's drift, McClaren frowned. "Far as I can see, none of that was Maggie's fault."

"She thought—she was married," Joe Ed said, with an effort.

"Yes sir. She told me."

The thick gray brows lifted in surprise. "Huh! That's a surprise—shows she trusts you. Ah"—he hesitated—"did she tell you who the man was?"

McClaren stirred uneasily. "Mr. Whitley, why are you bringing this up? I don't much like discussin' a lady's private business."

"I got a reason. Humor me."

Jess sighed. "All right. But first, one thing I'd like to know. If you don't want to answer, let it drop." He contemplated the hard palm of his right hand, then looked up. "Why in hell would your boy do a thing like that to Maggie—and to you?"

Whitley's face might have been carved from some ancient, seamed piece of oak, the emotions cut plain into it. There was pride there, and humiliation, and a sorrow too private to look at.

"I'll answer you honest, Jess. I am wholly to blame. I spoiled my boy. You see, I wasn't a young man even when he was born. My wife was just a girl, and pretty as a yearling filly. I never knew why she married an old loner like me. When our son was born, I was the proudest man in the country.

"Danny was a fine, sturdy little feller—like Joey! And his smile would charm birds off trees, McClaren. I couldn't never say no to him. Whatever he wanted, I saw he got it. After we took in that little baby girl, Maggie, I thought I had everything a man could want.

"But Danny's ma wasn't satisfied out here. Maybe I should have seen to it that she got into town more often. But I was worried she—well, the younger men took to her, you know—"

He trailed off, embarrassed. Jess waited without comment.

Whitley cleared his throat roughly. "By the time Danny was twelve, he was out o' hand. I caught him in some lies, caught him taking money from my strong-box. Anna wouldn't hear of my whippin' him. She was ready to scratch my eyes out if I so much as raised my voice to the boy. I saw where he was headed, and I should have put a stop to it. I just couldn't face up to his ma. There ain't no excuse for it, I know that well." He took a deep breath, seemed to gather his thoughts.

"When Daniel was sixteen, I knew I'd have to curb him. Worst thing was, he was makin' up to Maggie, even then, trying to coax her into the barn loft, and to ride alone with him." His big jaw tightened. Jess saw him clench his fist convulsively.

"He was too big fer me to lick, by then. By God, when I first realized his intentions, I wanted to take a horsewhip to him! I warned him never to lay a hand on Maggie again. I started to talk serious to my girl. Anna wouldn't do it, said Maggie had teased Daniel, that that little, innocent girl was a natural-born tramp!"

Heavily, he sighed. "I done my best to warn Maggie. The thing was, she worshiped that young devil of mine, and no wonder. He's a handsome man, McClaren. Black, curly hair, blue eyes like his ma's. Maggie loved him, and she was too young to know how he spent his evenings in Tularosa."

Whitley seemed short of breath. McClaren spoke up. "I know the rest of it. Maggie said after he tricked her, you ran Daniel off the ranch. She believes he'll be back one day. She plans to leave when that happens."

Whitley's face turned red. "Leave here?" he rasped. "Didn't you tell her the ranch will be hers?"

"Now, don't get a burr under your saddle, Mr. Whitley. You hadn't given me leave to talk about that to no one."

Whitley calmed himself, with a visible effort. "I've no doubt Daniel would try and move in on the place when I'm six feet under, if he thinks he can get away with it."

"Where is he now?" McClaren asked.

"God he'p me, I don't know. Don't want to know! I heard rumors he's been down in Mexico. The Rangers was after him a year ago, said he shot down an unarmed man, though I don't believe he'd do a thing like that. Maybe he's afraid to show his face around here. I hope to God he is."

Whitley fell silent. McClaren assumed the talk was over and rose to go. Whitley waved him back to his seat. "Wait. I ain't said what I meant to. It ain't the easiest thing, but you've made it some easier. McClaren, I *got* to provide some protection for Maggie an' the boy after I'm gone."

"If you've left the ranch to her legal—"

"I took care of all that six years ago. But you know as well as I do that a single woman is fair game. Now there's this here rustling. It'll only get worse after I'm underground. They'll wipe Maggie out, and she'll be forced to sell for half what the spread is worth. I don't mind her selling. I want her to do whatever she wants. But I know close to a third of my cows is gone already. Maggie's inheritance is slidin' through my fingers like sand."

"I aim to find out who's doing the rustling and put a stop to it," Jess reassured him.

The gray head shook. "That still won't stop some drifter with a glint in his eye moving in to sweet-talk Maggie out of what's hers and the boy's."

McClaren grinned. "Maggie don't strike me as the kind who could be sweet-talked very easy."

Whitley was not amused. "If you think that, you

don't know her! You seen her strong side, and thank the Lord she's got a backbone. You ain't seen her tender heart. The man Maggie loves could have anything she's got or ever will have."

"I think you underestimate Maggie, Mr. Whitley. She's seen what men can be like. She won't be fooled twice."

Whitley was silent a long moment, then fixed McClaren with his faded eyes. "Jess, I can't die peaceable until I can be sure Maggie and the boy will be all right. That's why I'm humbling myself now. I got no choice but to ask you right out. Will you keep Maggie safe? Will you marry my girl?"

Chapter Eight

Taken completely by surprise, McClaren stared at Whitley without speaking. When he could gather his thoughts, he shook his head slowly. "You shouldn't ought to ask a thing like that, Mr. Whitley, sir."

Whitley's eyes narrowed. "You think you are too good for a girl who—"

"Don't say it!" Jess's voice was dangerous, although it had not risen. "Don't say it, and don't think it. It's because I have respect for Miss Bourne that I'm telling you, you're making a mistake."

"How so?" He was gruff.

Jess sighed. "Maggie can't be handed over like a sack of oats or a likely cowpony. You can't just make some man a gift of her. In the first place, she wouldn't go for it—"

Whitley raised a tremulous hand. "She'd do what I ask. She knows I want what's best for her."

"Maybe she would, sir, and maybe she wouldn't.

But she'd feel cheated all her life, and if you think a little, you won't do that to her."

"Hogwash! Why should she feel cheated? You're the kind of man she needs! Why, I knowed your father for years, and I've watched you since you come here. Son—"

Jess interrupted. "I'm noways sure I'm good enough for Maggie! But that's neither here nor there. Women like to be courted, to be wanted for themselves and not for what they own or will own. Same as a man. They've got to have some say about it."

"Are you sayin' you couldn't love Maggie for herself, but only for this ranch?"

Jess felt like roaring with frustration. "No sir, I am not! But people hereabouts would think that. And Maggie would never know, maybe, how much she is worth."

"I thought maybe you and Maggie could see something in each other," muttered Whitley.

"Don't know what she'd see lovable in me." McClaren grinned. "As for Maggie, I'll tell you freely. If she *wasn't* about to inherit this spread and all the things I can't give her, I'd have asked her already if she could maybe care for me. But I've got nothing except my pride, and I'm not about to lay that down. Nor would you, in my place."

Joe Ed stared at Jess for a moment, then put out a work-hardened hand. "Anyways, I wasn't wrong about you, son. I just wish I could talk you into making my Maggie and her boy safe before I close my eyes for the last time. I believe you'd take care of her and be good to her. But I reckon you are right, she'd think she was the purchase price of the J-bar-W." He shook his head sorrowfully. "Sometimes I think I'd ought to have let the coyotes and mountain lions have this place, years ago. It's all I have to leave the ones I love best, but maybe after all it ain't nothing but a curse to them." His face settled into lines of sadness.

"Mr. Whitley, it's a fine place, and one day Joey will be proud of it."

Whitley nodded, but his face was weary. McClaren gripped Joe Ed's shoulder, then quietly left the room, leaving the old man to his thoughts.

* * *

Jess was preoccupied at supper, unable to shake off thoughts of his talk with Mr. Whitley. He found it hard to keep his eyes off Maggie, who moved about the kitchen, tall and graceful. Once she met his eyes and he felt a knot as big as a boot in his stomach. Was he as big a fool as he suspected not to have jumped at Whitley's suggestion? Here was a woman in a hundred. Most men wouldn't have objected to her future prospects.

But it mattered to him. And he'd have felt like a damned fool, making up to Maggie just to put window dressing on a deal already made behind her back. For that matter, he wasn't so sure he could ever break down that icy reserve she wore like a shield.

Unconsciously, Jess frowned at the vinegar pie on his plate. He had made the right decision. No use going over and over it. But how did he go about keeping his mind off Maggie Bourne?

After eating, he ambled down to the corral. Red followed.

"Friend, you look like a man with something on his mind."

It wasn't something he could talk about. Jess substituted a rundown of what he had learned from George Owens.

"Gabaldon! Nah, I doubt it."

"You know the man?"

"Heard of him. He worked with a gang of cow thieves that hole up in El Paso—or sometimes Socorro. They say he totes trouble with him like his own shadow."

"Owens believes he's hiding out in the Jornada. I'm going in to look for him tomorrow."

Warren stared at him. "Alone? Man, if you had the dumb luck to find him you'd get your head blowed off! That place is workin' alive of owlhoots who'll shoot a stranger and then look to see was he wearin' a badge."

"I need to talk to Gabaldon."

"Maybe you need a nice, shiny new headstone too!" Red snorted. "Gabaldon does his talking with a forty-four. Was you expecting him to invite you to tea, and have a nice, cozy gossip with you."

Jess grinned. "Not exactly. Listen, if he's workin' Whitley's herds, we've got to know who he rides for. Owens says Gabaldon couldn't have planned this deal for himself. Says the man isn't clever enough. And if he's just a two-bit owlhoot, what reason would he have for trying to push Joe Ed to the wall."

Red shrugged. "Gabaldon won't talk, even if you find him."

"You got a better idea?"

Red shook his head. "No sir, but that don't alter what I said. Gabaldon will put an end to all your worries, forever." He gave a wry grin. "An' just when I was gittin' to like you too. Well, do me one favor. Cross the basin at night. And wait a few days until you're healed up good."

Jess shook his head. "I've already waited too long. I'll start at sunset tomorrow."

Red made one further suggestion, that Jess take the bay stud, but only as a packhorse, to begin with. "He'll maybe get you out of there, where a ordinary cowpony couldn't. Maybe a pack saddle will disguise him enough you won't get plugged fer the horse."

At dusk the next evening Jess slipped away from the ranch on a compact and sturdy brown gelding. Capitan brought up the rear under a light pack, seeming a little surprised at the switch in status. No one but Red knew Jess was leaving, or his destination.

It was a sweet evening. Sunset spread washes of purple and brilliant gold beyond the San Andres. The blue mists of night settled into the valleys.

The brown gelding was short-gaited, but his sturdy legs were tireless. He struck a rapid fox-trot toward the mouth of Venado Canyon. Jess's side, stiff at first, soon adjusted to the horse's motion.

On the flats McClaren pushed the gelding to a lope. The brown was a young horse, fresh and lively. He made good time across the desert, finding his way among the humpy growths and in and out of arroyos.

The Mal Pais, a black, tumbled wasteland of lava, lay before Jess now, miles wide. The going here was bad. There was no trail, and it was the devil's own work to pick a way among the chaotic, upthrust slabs of once-molten black rock, and the yawning, treacherous chasms it had formed in cooling, centuries ago.

Jess was forced to walk and lead his horses. The darkness made it a harrowing business. Often, he had to backtrack to find his way out of an impasse. At last he stumbled into a faint deer trail, which took him in the right direction. Even so it was long hours before he broke clear of the desolate area.

By dawn McClaren had reached the foothills of the San Andres. He found a sheltered narrow canyon that showed no sign of the passage of any living thing, and made a dry camp.

He staked the brown, removed Capitan's pack and hobbled him. Then Jess slept for a few hours, waking when the midday sun grew too hot for comfort in the gully.

Checking first on the horses, who stood dozing in the shade of a scrubby piñon, Jess studied his back trail. Nothing moved as far as he could see in the heated stillness of the Tularosa Basin. Even the desert creatures were holed up, awaiting evening's relief from the sun.

Satisfied at last that he was alone, Jess risked a tiny fire, made coffee and chewed some venison jerky, then caught up the horses and was on his way again.

He had judged his route well. He was only a half mile from Mockingbird Gap. He spurred the gelding into the climb, hoping he looked as if he belonged here.

If there were watchers on the ridges, no one showed himself. He kept his saddle gun in its scabbard, feeling that it would be better to appear confident before the guardians of this hidden country.

No one challenged him as he followed the winding wagon track at a comfortable trot. He reached the top, stopped to rest and give the horses a taste of water from his canteen. He'd have to find a water hole soon or be in trouble.

Jess looked out over the forbidding vista. Rough slopes, dry rocky earth covered with pine, juniper, cedar, and other growth. Here and there a small grassy meadow lay golden in the afternoon sun. Far below the cool heights began the Jornada del Muerto, a burning, sun-cracked expanse that according to Warner was some fifty miles across, ending in the Rio Grande to the west. Lengthways the Jornado ran a hundred miles north from San Marcial to Doña Ana. It was largely waterless. Even in a good year it was not a place a man would lightly choose to be.

Jess rode at a leisurely pace down into the edge of the desert, then turned north to move along the edge of the foothills. Dwellings would mostly be found, Owens had hinted, in the canyons on this west side of the San Andres, where there would be water for men and livestock.

It was nearing dusk when McClaren found a canyon that showed signs of traffic by horses and wagons. He rode east, climbing again. Frowning, he glanced back at the bay stud. The horses were suffering for water.

He kept his horses at a trot, feeling exposed. Jess thought of Red's habit of riding the ridges. But he must play the part of the innocent and ignorant traveler if he hoped to approach the shy dwellers of the Jornada.

He topped a hill and saw a small rock cabin, sheltering against a sheer stone bluff. Jess stopped the horses and studied the scene from the concealment of a grove of oaks where the road bent.

He made out a human figure—surprisingly, a woman. She stood near a pile of dirt and a crude windlass, a rifle in her hands. Jess, puzzled, watched until he saw the woman lay aside the gun and go to work on the windlass, straining to pull a bucket out of a hole in the ground.

When she dumped a bucketful of dirt, he realized that someone was digging a well. The woman was standing guard for the digger.

Quietly Jess urged his horse into the open.

"Hello!" he called. "Anybody to home?"

At once the business end of the rifle swung his way, steady in the woman's hands.

Jess rode slowly to allow the woman to get a good look at him. He surmised from the motions of her head that she was speaking urgently to the well-digger, out of Jess's sight in the well. After a moment she advanced a few steps.

"Stranger, pull up. Put up your hands and stay where you are," she shouted.

Jess obliged. After a few moments' wait, a hatless head appeared at the level of the ground. Jess knew he was being examined. Doubtless there was a pistol on him as well as the woman's rifle.

"Who are you?" the woman called.

"McClaren's the name. From Texas."

The woman kept the gun on Jess until her companion climbed from the well and took the rifle, holstering his handgun. He walked closer to McClaren.

"Take off yore hat," ordered the middle-aged, balding man, who wore a drooping black mustache.

Jess obliged.

"I don't know you," stated the well-digger.

"No sir, reckon you don't" was Jess's amiable reply.

"From Texas, you say? The law after you?"

Jess was tempted to let the man think so, but he'd always found it hard to keep up a lie.

"Not that I know of," he replied thoughtfully.

"What brings you here?" The man's voice was cold.

"I'm trying to locate a man. His name is Gabaldon. I was told he would be somewhere in this area."

There was a long silence, then the well-digger spoke slowly. "You don't look like a lawman."

Jess shrugged. "I got no badge."

"What you want with this—Gabaldon?"

"I could say that's my business." Jess did not let his eyes waver when the rifle barrel lifted tensely.

After a long, taut moment, the man nodded. "I reckon you are right. I don't ask into another man's business."

"In that case, I'll tell you why I want Gabaldon." Jess smiled. "He tried to get away with a bunch of my boss's cows recently. You might say Gabaldon and I exchanged greetings, engraved in lead. I hear he's holed up in here somewhere, healing from my bullet."

"You come to finish the job?"

Jess sighed. "Likely I'll have to try, if he's as quick

on the trigger as seems his nature. But all I want from him is a name. Somebody is trying to ruin a sick old man who has worked hard and fought hard to hold his spread. Somebody smells his helplessness and means to get at his throat like a lobo wolf on a wore-out range bull. I got to find out who is so interested in preying on Mr. Whitley."

The man's eyes changed. "Whitley, you said. Would that be Mr. Joe Ed Whitley?"

"The same."

The rifle lowered. "Can you prove you are working for Joe Ed?"

"This horse carries his brand, if that's any proof."

The man with the rifle grinned suddenly with stained teeth. "Not likely, in these here parts. What the hell, I believe you, McClaren. Git down. My woman will make us some dinner."

"Thank you, mister. I take that kindly."

McClaren dismounted, loosened the cinch to let the gelding relax, watered both horses in the meager stream. He tied them near the cabin.

The balding man motioned his woman inside the house. He offered a dipper of water from a bucket on the porch to Jess. McClaren drank gratefully.

"I see you're diggin a well." He gave back the dipper and sat on the step.

"I never thought there'd be need. We got a spring, but it's mighty low. Never seen a worse drought."

Politely the two men discussed the lack of rain. Jess knew better than to ask his host's name. After a while the woman, her dark hair freshly combed and knotted at her neck, her strong, sun-browned face scrubbed, asked the men in to eat, as shyly as if she had not earlier menaced the guest with a rifle.

The food was good, if plain; fried venison with water gravy, hot biscuits, and molasses.

When the meal was done, the woman slipped out the back door of the one-room house. Jess weighed the risks, then asked about Gabaldon once more.

His host's dark eyes were grim. "I'd purely like to help you, McClaren. Whitley was more'n decent to me once. He give me a meal an' a safe place to lay my head and asked no questions. But I cain't, and I'm tellin' you the why of it. Only one way a body can survive hereabouts. That's to keep his mouth shut no matter how good a excuse he has to flap his gums. Take my advice. Put lots of ground between you and the Jornada. Most hombres in these parts won't invite you to quit your saddle, they'll blast you out of it from ambush. Strangers ain't wanted in here."

McClaren nodded, stood. "I'll be on my way. I'm obliged for the meal. Good luck with your well."

"I thank you."

McClaren went out to his horses. The shadows were long now, dusk closing in on the Jornada. He tightened his cinch, swung up, and turned the horse's head downcanyon, with Capitan trotting on the lead rope. Jess would have to find a place to camp soon.

He was just out of sight of the rock cabin when a sound in the brush startled the brown horse. He reared and came down sideways, back humping for more action.

Jess drew his Colt even as he yanked the tough-mouthed horse to a standstill.

"Don't shoot, mister!" came a harsh whisper. It was the woman from the house up the canyon. She faded back into the growth. "Keep riding slow, mister, and listen to what I got to tell you."

She trotted along just inside the concealing brush, panting out instructions.

"Ride a mile north. There's—a dead pine. Turn up that gully—'bout—five mile. Don't say I told."

"Why are you telling me?" McClaren asked softly.

"Gabaldon's right mean—to his woman—and kids." She vanished into the rustling leaves.

McClaren nudged the horse into a trot.

He found the dead pine and reined his horse into a steep, winding gully that looked too narrow and choked for anything but a weasel to slip through. It was dry and rocky, but McClaren spotted sign that horsemen had come this way, several days past.

He glanced at the sun, calculated that there was still

daylight enough to ride the five miles. He left the gully for the mountain slope. It was time to ride as silently and secretly as possible.

He found a game trail high on the forested side of the hill, and followed it until he judged he'd come four miles, keeping parallel to the dry wash. Walking the horses, he moved cautiously forward until he could see down into a grassy clearing dotted with pines. Against the far hill squatted a ramshackle log cabin. Most of the chinking was gone and the roof sagged. Three horses stood inside a tiny pole corral at the far end of the shack, eating some moldy-looking grass hay.

McClaren moved his horses back along the trail and tied them securely, then crept forward to look over the situation.

He saw no one. Smoke rose from a rusty stovepipe. McClaren could smell salt pork frying.

Jess began to work his way down to the trail that led to the cabin. He decided to circle the dwelling, climb the hill behind it, and toss his jacket over the stove flue, to smoke out whoever was within.

He did not get a chance to put his plan into effect. A clear young voice spoke behind him.

"Put up your hands, mister!"

McClaren cursed under his breath. He'd been caught in the open. Before he could see who had the drop on him, the door of the cabin burst open. A bull of a man stepped out, gun in hand.

"Stand still, mister, please." The whisper behind Jess was urgent.

"Who is it? Who you got, Eduardo?" shouted the big man.

"I do not know him."

"No matter, he got no business here." The big dark man leveled his Colt at McClaren. At the same time there was a sharp shove in Jess's back. "Fall down, mister!" hissed the boyish voice.

Instinctively McClaren obeyed, just as Pete Gabaldon's gun fired. Jess felt the wind of the bullet.

"You got him! You got him, Pete!" shrieked the boy, a skinny kid of about fourteen. "You better ride out, Pete!" the boy shouted excitedly. "I think there are other men with him. They must have heard the shot."

With a curse the man at the door whirled, limping, and ran for the corral. Another man darted from the cabin and joined him. After a moment Jess heard the slap of leather, and then the earth vibrated to galloping hooves.

"Lie still, mister," whispered the boy. "They will be gone soon."

McClaren stayed where he was until the boy signaled that he could get up.

"Come into the house. I will get your horses," he said as matter-of-factly as if he had not just now saved McClaren's life.

Inside the dim, odorous cabin, possessed of only one grimy window, a woman stood with hands pressed to her mouth.

Jess could see that once she might have been attractive, with large dark eyes and a round, innocent face.

Now her dress was too small for her plumpness, and her face was puffy. A greenish-purple bruise marred one cheek, another bruise showed where the sleeve of her dress fell back.

"Eduardo, what have you done?" she whimpered.

"Pete would have killed this man, Mama."

"He will find out! He will beat you, and me."

A little girl, thin and scared looking, her black hair stringy and uncombed, crept from a corner and huddled against the woman.

"Don't worry, Mama. Pete is running for his life." Eduardo laughed. "I will make a place that looks like a grave, and tell him this gringo is safely in it."

He turned to Jess. "I will get your horses. Wait here."

He slipped out of the cabin.

"Pedro Gabaldon is your husband?" Jess asked the woman. "These are his children?"

She shook her head violently. "No, no! *Los niños*, they are not his. He is not my husband. He—lives here sometimes."

"He beats you. Why do you let him come here?"

She stared at him, dull-eyed. "We are poor. Sometimes Pedro brings food."

McClaren brought out ten crumpled dollar bills. "Take this money and go away. Go to El Paso, or across the border."

She stared at the money as if it could not be real, then snatched it and thrust the money into her dress. Jess wondered if she would take his advice. Probably not. Women like this were victims by habit, with no courage to break that habit. Now and then one would be driven too far and take a butcher knife to the man who made life a hell. More often such a woman would simply endure the abuse, and the children would be trapped in the situation with her.

Uneasy in this close space, McClaren opened the front door. No sign of the boy and the horses yet.

There was sudden flurry of hoofbeats from behind the house. The back door was flung open before McClaren could do more than turn to confront Pete Gabaldon and a second man, both with guns drawn.

"See, Alfredo, didn't I tell you the boy was lying? Here is the gringo, waiting peacefully for us." He laughed, a high-pitched sound for such a big man.

"Put your gun away, Gabaldon. I only want to talk to you," McClaren said quietly.

The big man laughed wildly. "Do you hear the man, Alfredo? He asks me so nice to put away my gun. How is he going to make me do that, I wonder?"

He made a sharp, sidewise movement of his head to his companion, never shifting his eyes from McClaren. "Eduardo has probably gone for this fool's horse. Move ours well out of sight so the boy will not know we have returned. We will give the little traitor a surprise."

"*Pedro, no, no, por favor!*" pleaded the woman, tears streaming down her pendulous cheeks.

"You will keep still, woman, or I will cut out your black heart, as I should have done long ago. Your lying bastard will not lie to me again. He will not lie to anyone, and you may join him in death, if you wish. Go carefully to our guest and take his gun. Give it to me!"

She obeyed. Alfredo went out. Time crawled, with only the low sobbing of the woman to cut the stillness.

Having nothing to lose, McClaren spoke again. "Gabaldon, who pays you to rustle J-bar-W cattle? It's him I want, not you."

The big man made a peremptory gesture to silence. Jess knew that he was listening for the boy's return, and he felt cold inside. The kid had done him a favor. Would Eduardo pay for it with his life?

There was a thud of hooves outside. McClaren opened his mouth to call a warning—but there was the woman to consider, and the little girl. There would be bullets flying the moment he shouted.

The boy stepped in. He held Jess's rifle in his left hand. "Señor, you had better go, I think—"

His eyes had not adjusted to the dimness when Gabaldon brutally slammed him across the face with his pistol. As the boy's arms flung outward, Jess launched himself at the rifle. He caught it, hit the floor, gunfire already booming in his ears as he rolled. He had only an instant's aim, but the rifle slug hit Gabaldon in the chest. Jess shot twice more, once at the falling Gabaldon, once through the back door in case Alfredo had a taste for joining the battle.

Outside there was a sound of running feet, and then a horse raced away. Jess got to his feet. The fallen outlaw was dead, eyes wide and staring, lips drawn back in a snarl of surprised pain.

Quickly Jess looked for the others. The room was filled with smoke, acrid and choking. The stovepipe had been knocked apart. Eduardo lay still on the floor, curled up like a little child. His mother bent over him. The little girl stood staring, her face pinched with shock and fear.

"Come." McClaren pulled the woman to her feet. "I'll take him out of here."

Coughing, the woman and girl followed as he carried the boy's limp body between the cabin and the steep hillside, in case Alfredo was nearby, though it would soon be too dark for a rifleman to draw a bead on them. Within the partial shelter, Jess examined the boy.

"His face's cut some, but it doesn't look too bad."

"*Ah, gracias, ah madre de Dios!*" The woman wept, patting at the bloody, unconscious face of her son. Jess stepped out, scanning the darkening ridges tensely. Alfredo, he saw, had stolen Jess's J-bar-W gelding rather than taking his own poor specimen of horse flesh. The bay stud was still carrying the pack saddle, or doubtless the outlaw would have taken him, and nothing could have caught the bay this side of the border.

Jess could not detect anyone on the still canyon walls or the ridges. But there were many places to take cover, and the dark was thickening fast now. McClaren returned to the little family. Eduardo had opened his eyes. Blood ran from his raggedly cut cheek.

"Boy, do you think you can ride?" Jess bent over him.

Unsteadily, Eduardo sat up. "I think so, señor."

His mother rushed into the house, returning with rags and water to bathe her son's face.

"Listen to me," McClaren said urgently. "All of you must leave here, quickly. Take the horses Alfredo left. Eduardo, you must take your mama and sister far away from here. Alfredo might come back."

The boy nodded, his eyes more alert. "I have wanted to leave here many times. Mama was afraid of Gabaldon."

"He'll never bother you again. Get out of here as fast as you can." Jess grasped the boy's shoulder. "You saved my life today, son. If you ever need me, come to the J-bar-W, northeast of Tularosa. Miss Bourne or Mr. Whitley will know where I am."

"*Gracias, senor.*"

"One more thing. Do you know who was paying Gabaldon for stealing cattle?"

Eduardo shook his head. "Pete never told us nothing."

"Do you know who his friends are, or any place he meets his friends?"

The boy winced and pushed away his mother's ministering hands. "I saw him once with a man, where the trail comes into the canyon. A gringo, I think. The stranger did not come here. He rode south."

"Where did Gabaldon and Alfredo go when they weren't here?"

"Alfredo has a woman at a cantina in Las Cruces. It is called El Puerto Rojo."

McClaren stood. "Thank you, Eduardo. I'll leave my pack. You can have the food in it."

McClaren went into the cabin, found his Colt. Gabaldon stared blankly at death, his big body crowding the floor space. McClaren stepped past him and out the door. He stripped the pack saddle off the stallion, quickly twisted the lead rope into a hackamore and a rein, and swung up on the horse's back.

Capitan struck a long, easy trot down the canyon. It was nearly too dark to see the trail, but the bay's hooves rang unhesitatingly upon the iron-hard earth. The heat of the day was spilling away in the darkness.

McClaren reined in, got down to study the trail with the aid of a match. There were fresh hoof marks. Alfredo and the stolen gelding had come this way, at a pounding run.

"Ride fast, Alfredo," McClaren muttered. "Ride pretty damned fast, *amigo*, or I might be tempted not to let you make it to the cantina and your girl."

The stallion's hooves threw away miles of desert. The moon rose, and Jess lifted Capitan into an easy lope that the stud could keep up for hours, trusting the horse's good eyes to find safe footing.

McClaren rode all night. Just before dawn the horse smelled water and Jess let him find it, in a narrow fold of the foothills where nothing but animals had left marks of entrance. Nevertheless Jess's shoulder blades felt tense, and he scanned the wooded hillsides constantly as Capitan drank. It was a tiny, clear stream that flowed from a spring, a crevice in the granite fabric of the hills. When the horse had finished, Jess slid down stiffly and scooped a mouthful of cold water.

The bay grazed hungrily on the green weeds near the stream. McClaren decided to rest here. He led the horse upcanyon into a sheltered, grassy clearing. He hobbled Capitan with the rope rein and turned him loose, then made a bed for himself in the soft layer of needles under the low-spreading limbs of a piñon tree and was almost instantly asleep.

Chapter Nine

The sun was just beginning to filter into Jess's camp when he woke. Something had startled him from a deep slumber. He lay still, wondering what had roused him, fingers closing over the butt of his gun. For a tense moment he focused every sense upon his surroundings.

Then a squirrel chattered shrilly over his head. The little animal stared down at him, head tilted, tail twitching angrily as if demanding to know who dared invade his territory. It chattered another challenge at McClaren, then streaked lightly away up the tree. Jess relaxed and rolled out of his bed of leaves, brushing himself off.

He stretched and looked for Capitan. Hind foot cocked, the bay stud dozed near the stream.

Hunger twisted McClaren's stomach and he wished for coffee. He had to content himself with a drink of the spring water. He splashed his face, driving the last shadows of sleep from his mind. Regretting the loss of his saddle, Jess swung upon his horse and again made his way down to the desert.

From within the shelter of the little canyon, he looked out over the broiling noonday stillness. He could make out nothing but empty, heat-simmered distance. He kneed the bay into motion. Capitan trotted easily, gracefully weaving his way among greasewood and mesquite. Twice he passed near rattlers twined in the tough knee-high stems of sacaton grass.

McClaren heard their vicious buzzing with a tightening of his nerves. Like omens of what lay ahead, the snakes coiled and rattled in his mind long after Capitan's hooves left them behind.

At nightfall he approached the mining camp called Organ. To the east lay the fantastic, skyward-clawing sheer stone walls of the Organ Mountains, notched by San Augustin Pass. Westward the land fell away into the wide trough of the Jornada.

Avoiding Organ's cluster of buildings, McClaren swung westward toward Las Cruces, some fifteen miles. It was full dark when at last the sweated bay trotted into the dust of the town's streets.

Jess rode the length of the main street, a wide, treeless thoroughfare, lined on either side with low adobe store buildings and saloons, lamplighted. At the northern end stood the Sisters of Loretto Convent, an impressive red brick structure. A Catholic Church stood near the southern end of town. The road toward El Paso was paralleled by a dry *acequia*.

Jess found the cantina he was seeking on a narrow side street. Mariachi music, a rhythmic, wailing harmony of horns and guitars, poured out of the dingy saloon. Several underfed horses stood tied in front.

The brown gelding was not among them. Evidently Alfredo was a prudent man.

McClaren rode to the end of the street and turned in between a couple of shacks. He found the alley that ran behind the Puerto Rojo. The moonless darkness seemed to press against McClaren's face as he walked the stud quietly behind the buildings, passing evil-smelling pens and outhouses. He reined Capitan to a stop in the shadow of a small shed. A horse nickered inside. Horses and a wagon, then a couple of horsemen, moved past on the street at the end of the alley. Dogs barked somewhere on the edge of town. But nothing moved here behind the cantina. Jess eased off the bay's back, rifle in hand.

It took only the opening of a sagging shed door to find the J-bar-W gelding tied within, still saddled. Jess scratched a match and examined the horse. He had been ridden cruelly hard; his hide was rimmed with dried sweat, and he was drawn in the flanks. Alfredo had neither watered nor fed the horse. Cursing under his breath, Jess led the gelding out into the alley, quickly transferred the saddle and bridle to the bay, and jammed his rifle into the saddle scabbard. He slid Capitan's halter over the gelding's head, secured the brown horse to the saddle horn. Then he made his way through the littered backyard of the cantina to the rear door. Leaving it ajar, he moved across a dim, hot back room cluttered with wooden boxes and piles of empty bottles.

The music was loud and frantic. There were shouts and raucous laughter from the bar's patrons. Jess opened the door into the saloon a crack and peered in.

A girl danced in the middle of a room smelling of sweat and tequila. The space where the girl danced was surrounded by crowded tables. Her bright flounced skirts whirling, she twisted sinuously. Hands on hips, back arched, she smiled at the customers with rather pained determination.

Jess spotted Alfredo after a moment, alone at a table not far from the door where Jess stood. His swarthy face was oiled with perspiration. He grinned with broken teeth and waved a bottle to the beat of the guitars.

The girl held all eyes. She brushed near a customer with a suggestive thrust of shoulder and breast. The man made a grab for her. Onlookers roared with amusement as she slipped from his eager grasp, only to bring her seductive body close to another man.

McClaren seized the opportunity to slip into the smoky room, unnoticed. He laid his gun barrel against Alfredo's neck and bent to speak to him.

"You will come with me. Now. Or you are *muerto*."

Alfredo stiffened convulsively. His head, eyes rolling with alarm, twisted toward Jess, as his right hand jerked toward his shirt.

"You won't touch that knife, or your gun, if you want to see the sun rise tomorrow," Jess warned. "Get up and walk through that door. Now!"

Alfredo obeyed. In the dark back room McClaren took Alfredo's weapons and shoved both in his own belt. "Hands over your head! Step outside—slow, *amigo,* slow!"

With a handful of grimy collar, Jess thrust the man out into the hot night. He prodded Alfredo into the alley.

"*Por favor,* do not kill me," whined Alfredo. "I didn't do you nothing. It was that Gabaldon."

"I won't kill you if you tell me who was paying Gabaldon to run off Whitley's cows."

"Wheetley? Who is Wheetley?" The man's quavering voice rose frantically. "I don' know nothing about no cattle, señor, *por Dios*! I tell you *verdad.*"

There were hoof beats coming along the alley. Instinctively, McClaren glanced toward the sound. It was a mistake.

The Mexican twisted free and vanished into the darkness with no more noise than a fleeing rat.

Jess cursed under his breath. No use to linger here now. Alfredo might be back, with friends.

He untied the stud and mounted. Spurring Capitan into a trot, he rode toward the oncoming horseman. The brown gelding kept pace behind.

"Howdy," he muttered as he passed the cowboy. The other turned his head curiously as McClaren passed.

Jess rode through a section of small houses. Behind adobe or pine walls babies cried and hardworking people ate their simple evening meals. Jess felt suddenly more lonely than ever in his life.

Once clear of the town, he found a windmill, watered the horses. Mounting, he turned eastward, put Capitan to a ground-eating trot. He rode through the night, driven by an urgency that had nothing to do with J-bar-W cattle or rustlers.

He spent the hours intent in thought. The bay carried him over the steep climb and descent of the San Augustin Pass, through the rocky foothills of the Organs, and north and east to the edge of the White Sands. The Sands gleamed ghostly pale in the rising moonlight, an unearthly sight, the dunes seeming almost to rise and fall like ocean waves. Something about the scene was unnerving. Jess remembered stories he'd heard of murdered men left to rot within the white wasteland. McClaren wasn't a man to ponder the possibility of restless spirits, yet he skirted the Sands tonight, and even the tired gelding he led seemed to voluntarily quicken his pace.

He rode into the ranch yard at midmorning. Joey was playing with the ranch dog. He came running.

"McClaren!" he yelled.

"Hi, son. Where's Red?"

"Down to the corral, shoeing my pony. Can I ride Capitan to the stable?"

"Sure." Jess dismounted, set the boy in the saddle and gave him the reins. "These horses are tired, Joey. Walk 'em, and pen 'em away from water until they're good and cool. You can throw some hay down for them. No grain, I'll do that."

McClaren handed the gelding's lead rope to the child, who clucked proudly to the bay thoroughbred and bounced away.

"Mr. McClaren. You're back!"

Maggie was standing in the open front door. Jess felt his fatigue vanish as he met her eyes. Her face was anxious. She colored, started to speak, then stopped.

"Hello, Maggie."

She came down the steps. McClaren longed to put his arms around her. He could imagine how her hair would feel against his lips, and her slender body pressed close—

"We—we were worried about you," she said, her voice low and shaken. "I made Red tell me where you'd gone, Mr. McClaren."

He grinned. "Hey lady, if you know me well enough to worry 'bout me, you must know me well enough to call me by my given name."

There was no answering smile on her slim, tanned face. Her wide eyes were shadowy with distress. "You went into the Jornada del Muerto. No one but outlaws dares to ride in there."

"Then I must have looked like I had a posse on my tail, because I rode in and out again."

"Don't joke, please. You took a dreadful chance."

He dared to lay a hand on her shoulder. She did not

move away from his touch. "You can see I've come to no harm, Maggie."

"Jess—please promise you won't go to the Jornada again."

"I'd promise you anything for a hot meal and a few hours sleep."

"I'm sorry! Come in at once. I'll find some food."

While McClaren was eating, Warner came in, face red and beaming. "McClaren, you son of—oh, beg pardon, Miss Maggie. Jess, you are sure a sight for sore eyes. I'd about made up my mind to go hunting for you."

Jess grinned. "You wouldn't have found me. I've made a big circle."

Warner dropped into a chair. "Find out anything?" he asked, too quietly for Maggie to hear.

"Not much."

"You didn't find Gabaldon, then?"

"I found him all right."

"Yeah? Where is he?"

"I left him on the floor of a cabin on the west side of the San Andres."

"Dead?"

McClaren nodded.

"He talk before—" Red stopped as Maggie came to refill Jess's coffee cup.

"Would you like more steak?" she asked.

"No thanks, Maggie." God, how beautiful she was at this moment, her face warm with color from the heat of the stove, hair richly gleaming.

"Then I'll help Manuela with the wash."

Jess's eyes followed her as she left the room until he realized Warner was watching him with shrewd amusement.

Jess was suddenly irritated with Warner. And with himself. He'd better be more careful not to let his feelings show.

"Did you get anything out of Gabaldon?" Red repeated urgently.

McClaren shook his head. "He had the drop on me. By rights it should have been me needing a gravedigger. I had one chance. I took it."

"Then you still don't know who was paying him." Warner gave an odd sigh, his head bent thoughtfully.

"I had Gabaldon's pard collared back of the Puerto Rojo in Las Cruces. I was about to pry the truth out of him. Damned slippery little weasel got away from me in the dark."

Red leaned back in the kitchen chair, hands behind his head. "What's the next move?"

"Damned if I know, Warner. Right now I want to sleep for twelve hours straight."

Warner grunted and stood. Spur rowels ringing, he sauntered to the screen door, where Joey stood with chubby hands ringing his eyes, peering in.

"Hey Red," the boy demanded. "You said you'd take me for a ride soon as you finished shoeing my pony. You ain't finished yet. Hurry up, Red!"

Warner pushed open the door and ruffled the child's hair. "What's your rush? Cain't a man straighten his back for a spell without you got to whine?"

He and the boy disappeared in the direction of the corrals.

McClaren pushed back his chair as Maggie came in, carrying a laundry basket.

"All right if I turn in for a while?" he asked her.

"Yes of course. Get all the rest you can."

He placed his hands on the back of his chair and pushed it back up to the table, then stood holding it. He had the feeling that if he lifted his hands they would reach of their own accord for hers. He found that he did not want to break the contact of his eyes from hers, and when he turned away, he felt like cussing a blue streak. What had fate got against a man, that it could tempt him with a prize like Maggie and at the same time fence him away from her? Jess had been content to be alone, before he met Maggie Bourne. He would never know that old contentment again. No matter where he rode, he would feel this hunger gnawing at his guts, this ache to turn back to Maggie.

Within his room he shucked off his dirty shirt, took off spurs and boots, and laid his long body on the bed.

He was asleep almost before the feather pillow had sunk beneath his head.

The supper bell woke him. He discovered that while he slept someone had covered him with a light woolen blanket, the bright weave soft against the bare brown skin of his chest.

Had Maggie's strong, slender hands spread the cover over him? The thought brought a surge of passionate longing. Jess clenched his jaw and threw the blanket back almost angrily. He was in danger of making a damned fool of himself if he couldn't curb his thoughts about Maggie.

He reached for his boots, yanking them on over socks that were wrinkled and dirty. What he needed was a wash and clean clothes. Then he might feel human enough to face the world.

Joey was in the corridor. When Jess stuck his head out of the bedroom, the child was seated on the hall floor, whittling a pine stick all over the carpet. He looked up sulkily.

"Son, would you ask Manuela for some hot water?"

The boy shook his head morosely. "Can't. Maggie said not to wake you up."

Jess grinned. "You didn't wake me up. Man's got to get up sometime, anyway."

Within minutes Manuela was bustling along the hall with clean towels and a steaming teakettle, beaming at McClaren. "I'll bring a clean shirt, Señor McClaren. We wash two for you today."

"Thanks, Manuela. I feel like a rained-on saddle blanket."

As soon as she left, he poured the water in the basin, lathering the yellow bar of soap over his upper body.

He was washing his face, rinsing the dust of days away, when there was a soft step behind him.

"I brought—oh, I'm sorry!"

McClaren straightened and turned, drying his face.

"Please excuse me," Maggie said, flustered. "Manuela

said you needed a shirt, and I—" She stumbled to a halt, her cheeks pink.

All Jess's good sense abandoned him. He made one stride and caught her close. Her face turned up to him, wonderingly, and he claimed her lips with all the pounding urgency of his blood. His fingers touched the flesh of the nape of her neck and the silky coil of hair confined there. He longed to drag the pins from her hair and let it tumble down, to bury his face in the fragrant mass. He could feel the response of her lips, warm and yielding under his, as her body trembled in the circle of his arms—

He lifted his face, aware that he broken all his good resolutions. He had broken his own barrier, built so carefully.

She gazed up at him, breathless. "Jess, I—"

"McClaren, ain't you ready to eat yet?" Joey demanded, trotting into the room.

Hastily Maggie pulled away from Jess, turned to her son. "Joey, you mustn't bother Mr. McClaren when he's dressing!" she scolded.

Joey regarded her, round-eyed. "Why can't I, Maggie? You are, and he don't care."

"It's all right, son," Jess intervened, not sure whether to laugh or cuss.

Triumphantly, Joey darted around his mother. She laid the shirt on the bed and went out, carefully avoiding Jess's gaze.

Jess pulled on the shirt, hurried on by the hungry child. They went along the hall to the kitchen, Joey pounding ahead. McClaren hesitated in the doorway, surprised and pleased to see Joe Ed seated at the head of the plank table. Red and Curly came in and sat down, already reaching with forks to spear chunks of roast wild turkey.

Curly whistled. "Must be my birthday. Man, do I love turkey."

Manuela's boys settled into their chairs. "I shot that gobbler up in the willows this morning," José said.

"Hey pard," Warner teased Joey. "How come you're a-settin' over there with McClaren? I thought you and me was buddies."

Joey's mouth was too full to answer. He looked up at Jess doubtfully. Jess smiled. "He can't get a fair shake with the turkey if he sits between you and Curly."

"Maybe McClaren can teach that young hellion some manners, Red." Joe Ed chuckled. "He don't seem to git no polish from you fellers."

Red reached for a biscuit. "McClaren sure as hell ought to be rough enough to polish sandstone. He's done been in and out of the Jornada and he's all of a piece. Rode in there, cool as you please, and laid Pete Gabaldon low."

There was a startled silence in the kitchen as Red's words sank in.

McClaren's face went rigid, and he cursed inwardly. What was the matter with the man? Had he been drinking? It wasn't like him to let his tongue wag out of turn.

Joey was gazing up at Jess with awe, mouth open. Jess felt Maggie's shocked gaze and wondered what was going through her mind. Damn Red anyway.

"That true, McClaren? You tangle with Gabaldon?" Joe Ed asked.

Jess nodded shortly.

"Come on, McClaren." Warner grinned. "Don't be backward, man! Tell 'em how Gabaldon got the drop on you there in his woman's cabin, and—"

"Red, shut your trap," Jess warned evenly. "Or maybe I'll shut it for you."

"He's right," Joe Ed said at once. "This ain't a fit subject in front of women and children, nor at table."

The incident had changed the mood of the meal. The talk became subdued and uneasy now, and Jess felt the curious glances of Manuela's boys and Curly Brissom.

After supper, Jess wasn't surprised to be summoned to a private talk with Mr. Whitley. Briefly he described his confrontation with the rustlers. The old man, slumped in a rocking chair in Anna's carefully tended parlor, where he seemed completely out of place, turned his seamed face to Jess.

"What's your thoughts on this, McClaren? Now that Gabaldon is dead, will the raids on my cows stop?"

Jess met the rancher's eyes soberly. "I have been told that this operation wasn't likely planned by Gabaldon. But I didn't know the man long enough to make a guess on it." His smile was wry.

"But you got a gut feeling about it."

Jess shrugged. "Wellsir, if you ask me, it probably ain't over yet. And I'm wondering about something. Easy enough to run cows over the border with plenty of good water along the way. With this danged drought, where could the thieves water the herds that they wouldn't be spotted?"

"The same thing has struck my mind time and again." Whitley's faded eyes were intent on Jess's.

"The rustlers could be selling your beef to Fort Stanton, already butchered, or holding the cows this side of the border," Jess muttered, "in some isolated canyon maybe, where there's feed and water. Holding the cows and waiting. But for what?"

"For me to get boogered enough to sell out?" suggested the old man.

"Maybe. If that's what we're up against, the first ones to suspect may be neighboring cowmen. It would have to be someone near enough to make fast raids, get the cows away and hidden quick, no long drives to be remarked on. But why haven't your men been able to trail the stolen cows?"

Whitley shook his head. "Red could trail bluejay through a pine forest. He went out every time we knew or suspected that cows had been taken. Mostly we discovered the losses too long after to hope for any kind o' trail. But even when we knew a day or two after, Warner could only trail them so far. They must be carrying them cows on their backs, way they disappear!"

McClaren stared thoughtfully at the black iron parlor stove. He wasn't seeing the squat, neatly blacked stove, nor the chrome ornament on the top, the isinglass square of window in the door. He was visualizing the lay of the J-bar-W and surrounding territory as best he could.

"Clear Rivers land runs to the north of this spread?"

"Yeah. They got the best water in the area. That ain't to say they might not like a little more, in this drought."

"And Pardue is south?"

Whitley rubbed his scalp with gnarled fingers. "I've knowed Cal Pardue since we was both a hell of a lot younger. Cal's no cow thief."

"Still, I think I'll do a little riding on your neighbor's holdings, just to take a look-see," mused McClaren.

"Cain't hurt, I reckon, unless one of their hands take *you* fer a rustler."

"I'll undertake to look real innocent." Jess grinned. "Not too many folks know yet I'm working for you. I might see things that would be hidden from your other men."

Joe Ed nodded. "By the way, George Owens rode in while you was gone. I give him a job and he's gone back to town to pay his bill at the roomin' house and get his gear. He's like me, cain't work much anymore, but we had some good old times together, and it will be mighty welcome to shoot the breeze with an old friend."

"He did us a favor with his information about Gabaldon. Wish I could have made better use of it, got something out of Gabaldon before—he died."

Whitley studied him. "You don't much enjoy killin', do you son?"

McClaren shrugged. "I keep wondering if there might have been a better choice."

Whitley rubbed his jaw. "Some men don't give you no choice. I sent mor'n one like that to his maker, in my day. I never mulled it over much, after. I never hurt no man until he tried to do harm to me or mine. But I didn't let no one ride roughshod over me, neither. Don't let it lie too heavy on your mind, son. Some men is just born to be killed like the varmints they are."

"Reckon you're right." McClaren rose.

"Son, have you give any thought to what I mentioned the other day? About you and Maggie?"

As Jess frowned, Whitley raised a placating hand.

"I know, I wasn't to say no more about it. But I seen tonight how she looks at you, when you don't know it, and I seen how she paced from window to window while you was in the Jornada, and Lord only knew would you come back, or lie there in them hills for the buzzards to find."

"She'd worry as much about any of the hands, Mr. Whitley."

"I ask you to believe I know her some better'n that! Jess, Maggie cares fer you." He was silent for a long moment. "I see the horizon in your eyes, Jess. You gonna leave my girl behind when you light out?"

"I've got nothing to offer a woman," Jess said, low and harsh. He knew his pain was showing.

"Jest tell me this much," Whitley persisted. "Do you feel anything for Maggie, or is she alone in this?"

Jess had to meet the old man's eyes. The lie wouldn't cross his lips. He sighed.

"Mr. Whitley, I never was any great shakes at hiding what I feel. Maggie's all I'd ever want in a wife. But I can't go to her with empty hands."

Before Whitley could answer, Jess left the room, and the house, heading instinctively for the corrals.

Capitan had been turned out into the night pasture. The black mare was in a pen with two ranch mares. Jess compared the young mare, bred by one of Mexico's finest horsebreeders, with the sturdy mustangs in the same pen. There was something to be said for both. The J-bar-W mares were nothing special to look at, but they'd carry you all day and all night and all day again on a spoonful of water and a mouthful of grass. The black filly needed more care. But she was built for speed and her own kind of endurance, and she pleasured the eye as well. McClaren reckoned there would always be a need for both kinds of horses.

He climbed up, dropped over the fence, rubbing a hard palm over the mare's neck, thinking of the good colts he'd raise from this mare and, someday, others like her.

"She's lovely, Jess." Maggie spoke softly as she unlatched the gate and stepped into the pen. It was so right and natural that she be there with him that he hardly wondered at the way she had appeared without betraying her approach.

Maggie held a graceful hand to the black's curious nostrils and let the animal lip softly at her fingers.

"She was bred near Chihuahua. My pa and I had a little horse ranch in Texas, some good stock. We brought the stud and a few mares out of Mexico a year before Pa died."

"Where are the others now?"

He shrugged. "Pa was unlucky at the cards. After he died I sold the land, bought back Capitan and this filly."

"McClaren, I'm sorry. You must have hated leaving your home."

Her shoulder brushed his arm. He wondered at this new side of Maggie. She was talking to him like an old friend, with none of the hostility and suspicion she usually showed.

"Land belongs to the good Lord, not men," he said. "Some of us get to borrow it, for a time. Others take over when we die or move on."

"Will you be moving on, Jess?"

There was something in her quiet words that disturbed Jess's breathing.

He steeled himself. "I will," he replied, "when I've done what Mr. Whitley needs done. If I *can* do it. Haven't made much of a showing so far."

She ignored his attempt at changing the subject. "Do you like being alone, then? Are you one of those men who follow the sunset and hate the thought of settling down?"

He made himself grin. She smiled back, so naturally that he discovered a new ache in his chest, and almost wished she would resume her cool, forbidding reserve. "It's born in some men to have itchy feet, Maggie."

"But not all of them ride alone," she said, unsteadily.

He held his breath, searching his mind for words to send her away from his side before it was too late, before he forgot his pride and resolve again.

Incredibly, she lifted a hand to touch his cheek. "I was afraid for you while you were gone, Jess," she whispered.

He caught her fingers, holding them too hard, feeling himself driven beyond human endurance. He tried to make himself say the words that would send her away.

"*Will* you ride alone, Jess?" she asked, her voice little more than a whisper.

Jess was fighting a losing battle, knowing what it must have cost Maggie to come to him. It would not be merely a flirtatious move, not with Maggie's hard-minded honesty.

God, how to resist what this lovely woman offered? He was human, not some saint, above the needs of common men! Jess caught her close, bending his head to meet her lips. The sweetness of her lips was a fulfillment of a promise. Delight that bordered on pain wiped away all doubts in Jess's mind—for a moment.

A breath of sanity returned as she broke the contact. Reluctantly, McClaren stepped away from her. She seemed shaken, but her eyes were glowing with an inner light.

"Maggie," Jess said hoarsely, "this isn't right. I can't let you—"

She laid quick fingers on his lips. "Jess, when you go, we're going with you, Joey and I. Unless—" Her chin lifted proudly, defiantly. "Unless you tell me you don't want me, that you can't—can't love me."

She waited for his answer. He knew he had to draw back, maybe laugh a little, tell her he didn't plan on loving any woman and let himself be tied down, that powerful as the feeling was she kindled in him, it could be called by other names than love.

But her dark eyes were pleading with him. He knew his own face was revealing too much to her, that maybe even the cruel words wouldn't convince her she was nothing to him.

Jess drew in a hard breath. What did it matter? The words wouldn't let themselves be said. He could only move to her and hold her, absorbing the warmth and sweetness of her. He touched her face in the gathering dark, and found it wet with tears.

Abruptly he remembered that Maggie still had no idea that Joe Ed meant for her to have the J-bar-W.

What was she going to think when she learned that he *did* know? Would she believe that his talk of leaving was a deception?

There were footsteps in the dusk, the clink of spurs. McClaren stepped away from Maggie but it was too late. Red Warner passed the corral with a sidewise glance and a knowing grin. Jess cursed himself for letting Maggie be caught in such a compromising scene. If there was talk in the bunkhouse of this, he would knock some heads together.

He might have felt even worse had he known at that moment that Warner was not the only one who had witnessed their embrace.

Deep in the night, McClaren lay sleepless on his bed, still fully dressed, lamp turned low. His bedroom door swung silently open. Someone stepped in. In an instant, Jess was on his feet, gun drawn.

There was a light, tinkling laugh. "Mercy, Mr. McClaren. How you frightened me. Is this how you greet a lady?"

Jess drew a sharp breath and laid the gun aside. "What can I do for you, Mrs. Whitley?"

"Shh! Not so loud. I want to talk to you—privately. There is so little opportunity. You don't mind my dropping in like this?" Her expression was coy. She wore only a silk nightgown. Her light hair fell loose about her shoulders.

In the dim light, one might take her for a much younger woman. Her eyes sparkled with excitement, and she smiled widely when he did not answer.

She glided to the bed and seated herself. McClaren went to the lamp, turning it up.

"No, no, put it out!" she whispered urgently. "No one must know I'm here—you understand, don't you, Jess? Sit here beside me, so I can talk without shouting." Invitingly, she patted the counterpane.

McClaren hesitated, then drew a straight wooden chair nearer the bed and straddled it backward. "What can I do for you?" he asked coolly.

"Why—just answer my questions, please. I heard about the terrible fight you had with that outlaw, and I was so very frightened for you!" Her hand crept out to his knee.

Chapter Ten

Jess stood and moved away. Anna laughed softly, ruefully. "Indulge a poor woman, please, Jess. Tell me about the man you—killed." She gave a delicate shudder.

McClaren's irritation was growing fast. "There's nothing to tell. He tried to kill me. I got him first."

"He was the man who had been taking our cattle?"

"One of the men."

"You surely don't imagine there are others?"

McClaren caught a subtly hidden urgency in her question. "I think so, yes."

"But who? Perhaps you managed to make this man, Gabaldon, tell you?"

"No ma'am, but I aim to find out."

"How?" She rose and stood close to him. He could feel the warmth of her flesh through the thin stuff of her gown. "How will you find out? I am so—worried about you." She placed both hands on his shoulders. Her eyes were sunken pools of shadow in the small oval of her face. Her teeth glinted within her parted lips as she tilted her face beguilingly. Her breath was unsteady, and she began to stroke his cheek, above the beard.

"I am so very frightened for you, Jess," she said huskily. "Put your arms around me just for a moment. Reassure me."

Abruptly he stepped away. "You'd better go, Mrs.

Whitley. If you were seen coming from here, it might not look good."

"You mean, someone might think that you and I—" She laughed breathlessly. "Then let us make it the truth, Jess!"

She came and pressed her body against his, wrapping both arms tightly about him. Some scent in her hair rose strongly in his face. "I saw you with Maggie this evening," she whispered. "I can do for you whatever she can—and better, you'll see. Much better." She lifted her face to him, her panting breath soft on his cheek.

Roughly he took her hands from behind him and pushed her away. "You'd best go. Now!"

He opened the door and stood there, waiting for Anna Whitley to leave his room.

At that moment there was a shout from Joe Ed's room. The door burst open, and a man rushed out into the hall.

Instinctively McClaren leaped to intercept him, unable to see who it was. They crashed into one another. The man struck savagely at McClaren. The hard fist grazed Jess's temple.

Catching the intruder's arm, Jess hit back. His fist drove into the man's belly.

There was a grunt. The stranger sagged momentarily, but rallied too quickly for Jess to follow up the punch with another. He tried to twist away from McClaren's grasp.

Jess slammed him against the wall, but the man managed to raise a knee with a hard thrust. Jess stumbled back and caught a slamming blow on the chin. He found himself with one knee on the floor, head spinning on the edge of unconsciousness, as heavy boots pounded away.

Someone shrieked Jess's name and tried to pull him to his feet. His skull buzzed. Nausea rose in his throat. When his vision cleared a bit, the first thing he saw was the hem of Mrs. Whitley's gown and her slippered feet.

Painfully he brought his head up. Joe Ed was leaning unsteadily in his room doorway, white hair all on end. Maggie was beside him, in the hall, a lamp in her hand. Whitley was looking toward the window at the end of the hall, where the man had gone out. But Maggie's eyes were on Jess and the woman who tugged at his arm.

McClaren shook Anna's clinging fingers off and got to his feet.

"Who in hell was that?" he muttered thickly.

"I woke up—he was leanin' over my bed," Joe Ed mumbled.

"You okay?" Jess moved toward the old man. A shock like this might put him flat of his back again. Maggie evidently had the same thought, touching Whitley's arm anxiously.

Irritably, Whitley shook his head. "I'm fine. Don't make a fuss, Maggie."

Joey came trotting drowsily into the hall in his nightshirt. "Somebody's in the house!" he shouted. "I heard somebody in the house! Maggie!"

Maggie bent and gathered him close. "It's all right, honey. He—whoever it was is gone now."

Something in the way she said it alerted Jess. But she refused to look at him, gently coaxing her son back to his bed.

Mrs. Whitley was cooing something to McClaren. Rudely he turned on his heel and strode out into the night by way of the back door.

He made a round of the house, moving quietly from shadow to shadow, seeing no one until Red Warner came running from the bunkhouse.

"What's going on?" he shouted. "I heard a horse. Somebody lit outta here like a dog with a tomater tin tied to his tail!"

"Yeah." Jess rubbed a hand along his aching jaw. "He slipped into the house—he was in Joe Ed's room."

"What the hell! Sorry I didn't get here sooner," Red said. "Couldn't find my danged boot."

Until then it hadn't occurred to McClaren that Warner had taken a surprising amount of time to hear the ruckus and reach the ranch house.

Jess frowned, impatient with himself. What was it made a man's mind fasten onto unimportant matters when there were real problems his brain ought to be unraveling?

"Who would want to sneak into the house this time of night?"

Red shrugged and yawned widely. "Beats me. Well, if you don't need me, think I'll get some shuteye. What's on for tomorrow?"

Some unexamined instinct made McClaren cagey. "Can't say yet. Have to do some thinking."

Red muttered a good-night and ambled away.

Something was bothering Jess. Something he couldn't quite pin down—

It slammed into place in his mind. Maggie. The way she'd looked after the scuffle in the hallway. Oh, hell! She'd seen the way the Whitley woman's hands were all over him. Maybe she'd even seen Anna come out of his room.

Something deep in his soul groaned. How was he going to explain that? Anything he might say would sound like a convenient lie.

He went back into the house. Maggie was in the kitchen, pouring coffee for Joe Ed. She set a cup before Jess, not meeting his eyes.

Jess frowned at the black brew. He had to talk to her, and soon. From the way she was ignoring him, that might not be easy.

Joe Ed's eyes traveled from Maggie to him, with a knowing look. The older man stood, leaving his coffee half-finished.

"I'm for bed. That varmint won't be back tonight."

"I'll help you—" Maggie began.

"Land sakes, girl," Joe Ed snorted. "I ain't Joey's age! Leave a man his dignity, cain't you?" He grinned. "Think that gentleman at the table wants a word with you. You set down and listen to him."

Reluctantly, Maggie sank into a chair at the far end of the table. She wore a faded flannel robe over a high-necked nightgown. Her rich auburn hair was braided down her back in one thick plait, and she looked about seventeen. Her eyes were wide and troubled, but at least now they were meeting his.

He moved a chair near hers. "Maggie. What's wrong?"

"Wrong? Isn't it enough that someone broke into the house tonight, scaring us all out of our wits?"

He ignored her evasion as pathetically obvious. "Maggie, I have to know what's really bothering you."

She dropped her eyes for a moment, then looked up, her face still and blank. "Why was she in your room?"

He gave a long sigh. She was going to meet it head-on. Good.

"Mrs. Whitley was not invited to my room, Maggie, and she had been asked to leave before the commotion started."

She studied his face as if wondering if she dared believe him. He met her eyes steadily. At last she let her breath out like a tired child and reached her hand out to him. Jess blessed her honest heart as he caught her fingers. He looked down at her hand, opening it, touching a callus on her palm, tracing the length of her slim, strong fingers. This was a woman who never spared herself, a giving, caring woman.

"I'm—I'm sorry, Jess," she said. "I had no right to ask about it."

His voice was rough, uneven. "You have every right. Reckon you'll always have that right, where I'm concerned. I want you to believe me. That woman ain't welcome in my room—nor in my bed."

Her eyes widened at his bluntness, then she smiled faintly. "Not every cowhand on this ranch has felt that way."

"You thinkin' I'm just like every other cowhand?"

"No, I know you're not." Her smile remained, but he sensed that there was still something troubling her. After a moment's thought, he was fairly sure of his ground. Maggie was so easily read. It wasn't in her nature to hide anything.

"Maggie, you want to tell me now who our visitor was?"

Her head bent. "How did you know?" she whispered.

"That ain't important."

She sighed. "You're too quick for me, Jess McClaren."

"If you knew him, why didn't you just say so?"

She hesitated, then shook her head as if it pained her. "Because I wasn't sure what knowing would do to Joe Ed. It was his son. It was Daniel Whitley."

McClaren stiffened. "Are you sure?"

Her mouth thinned. "I ought to know."

"What would he be doing here?"

"Oh Jess, who knows? I suppose he thinks he has the right to come and go as he pleases. It's his home, or was. Before long it will belong to him."

That was not true, but she could not know it, nor could Jess tell her. "Joe Ed warned him never to come back."

"Danny," she said wryly, "was never one to take orders."

McClaren moved his half-empty cup, watching the swirl of the dark, steaming coffee. Suddenly he didn't want it, and he pushed it away.

"So—he's come back. Maybe for you and Joey."

"No!" Her nostrils flared.

"The boy is his son. No man worth his salt would give up his son."

"Man?" she breathed. "Daniel Whitley isn't a man. And he never knew he had a son."

Jess kept his voice even. "Maggie, he must know it, the way talk gets around."

She looked up at him with sudden intensity. The fear was displayed nakedly. "Jess, will he try to take Joey?"

"Over my dead body."

Maggie covered her face, bent her gleaming head to the table top and wept.

McClaren stood and pulled her into his arms, holding her like a child. Trembling, she clung to him.

He held her until she calmed, then led her to her room. "Get some rest," he advised. "Things will look better tomorrow."

Silently she nodded and left him.

Back in his own room, he shut his door solidly and set the wooden chair under the doorknob. It was the last time, he vowed, that Anna Whitley would enter his room while he was present.

In the act of removing his shirt, he hesitated.

It had been his intention to visit one of the neighboring ranches, come daylight. For some reason he couldn't quite name, he'd felt unwilling, after the disturbance of this night, to advertise his plans. In fact, he felt an increasing urge to keep those plans to himself.

So now might be a good time to slip away from the J-bar-W. If he was careful about it, he'd be far away from headquarters before anyone missed him.

Jess checked the load of his handgun and tied the holster down to his right leg. He picked up his spurs, shoved the rowels into his hip pockets to keep them from ringing. Taking up his coat and saddlebags, he blew out the lamp and slid like a long shadow from the window.

By sunup Jess was putting Capitan over the crest trail. As far as he could see to the eastward, fold upon fold of wooded canyons and magnificent peaks lay gilded with early light. Westward a man could see for a hundred miles, across the Tularosa Basin to the Mal Pais and its eerie companion, the White Sands, to the dim blue links of the San Andres and further north, the Oscura range.

It was a good country. It could get into a man's blood, the same way an auburn-haired girl with troubled dark eyes could. But it was not an easy land. It could trap a man and lead him to his death.

Up ahead, Jess caught the slow hoofbeats of a horse. Reminded that caution was more important than a weapon in these wilds, Jess reined the stud silently into a thick stand of piñons and sat listening. When he was certain it was a single horseman, he rode out of the trees to be in plain view of the rider when he came around the next bend in the trail.

He held Capitan still, prepared for anything. The stallion threw up his head and nickered as a lazily ambling mouse-colored mare moved into sight. The animal stopped in her tracks, overlong ears swiveling forward. The rider, who had been dozing in the saddle, jerked awake.

Jess relaxed, and rode nearer. "Howdy, Toland."

The man blinked, stared. "That you, McClaren? Man, you done skeered me out o' ten good years of living. At my age, cain't afford it. You'd best be careful, jumping a man thataway!"

Jess grinned. "That a coffeepot I see hangin' to your saddle? I'll build a fire if you can spare a man a bite of breakfast."

"I was just thinking to stop an' eat," admitted Toland. "I ain't had but a hour of sleep, and I'm plumb done in."

"You headed home?"

"Yessir. Had some business over to Mesilla. Camped back there aways last night late."

"How come you rolled out so early?" McClaren asked. "Sun's just barely up."

Toland gave a toothless grin. "I could ask the same of you, son." He turned his elderly mare to follow McClaren off the ridge and into a tree-shrouded gulch where a fire would likely not be noticed. The wind would carry the smoke off to the wild canyons eastward.

Jess got down and built a small fire, while Toland got out bacon and cans of beans, and a sack of Arbuckle's coffee.

"I was sleeping the sleep of the innocent," Toland drawled, "when some damn fool rode his horse most nearly over my camp, hell-bent for somewhere southwest. Spooked my mare, and I had to catch her up in the dark. I was some lonesome by that time, and all woke up, so I decided to git on fer home. They's some strange goin's-on in these hills. Man hears funny rumors. It don't pay much to ride the canyons alone no more."

McClaren nodded. "I feel eyes on my backbone even when I know there's nothing out there but wind and rock and a hungry hawk or two."

"What's the word from Joe Ed Whitley's place?"

McClaren told him about the latest raid on Whitley's cattle, his own ride into the Jornada, and, without detail, Gabaldon's death. "I'm at a standstill," he said. "I made up my mind to make a nuisance of myself on the neighboring spreads and see if I scare up anything."

"You're wondering if them neighbors could be a-tryin' to wipe Joe Ed out?"

McClaren frowned. "Be hard to shove a herd across the border with the drought hanging on. But those stolen cows have vanished like the smoke from this fire."

"Meaning, could they be hidden someplace in one of these canyons?" Toland nodded briskly.

He stopped to pour coffee into a tin cup and handed it to Jess, along with a tin pan of bacon and beans.

Jess had a feeling that there was something Toland wanted to say, but Toland was cautious.

"What's your notion, Mr. Toland?" Jess probed gently. "If you can steer me the right way, I'd appreciate it. They're in deep trouble on J-bar-W, trouble they don't deserve. Mr. Whitley's determined to hold what he's worked to build up, for Miss Maggie and her boy."

"Not fer his own son, huh?"

Jess kicked himself mentally. Had he made a mistake, letting this slip?

But Toland didn't seem disapproving. "That Maggie Bourne, now there's a fine young woman. I never held with folks turning against her when she had her trouble, nor against that little boy of hers. Cute as a speckled pup, that kid is." He gave a brisk little nod. "You know, Maggie come over when my woman was sick some months back, nursed her like a baby, and cooked and cleaned for us. Wouldn't take nothing fer it but a word of thanks."

"She's a—a special lady."

Toland chewed bacon and looked at Jess with eyes that were bird-bright. "Wellsir. I can't tell you much. I don't know much, nor do I want to. I will say this. Take it as you please. Was I you, I'd steer that good-lookin' stud over to Pardue's headquarters. Might be you'll see something. Might be you won't." He sighed heavily. "Might be if you ride in there, you won't ride out, an' some other feller will be forkin' that fine bay horse. Only the good Lord knows."

He snapped his mouth shut and stood to stamp out the fire and collect his gear. Jess knew he would say no more. He shook the older man's hand. "Much obliged," he said.

Toland shook his head doubtfully and climbed onto his mouse-brown mare, plainly anxious to be gone. He slapped the animal sharply on the rump and into reluctant motion.

Chapter Eleven

The sun soared high and bright over the mountains, intensifying the resinous scent of firs and the sharp, bitter smell of hoof-crushed weeds. Fine dust drifted in the hot breeze.

Jess rode at a leisurely fox-trot along the ridge. Down on the flats the day would be almost unbearably hot. Up here even the brassy sun couldn't make a man wish to be somewhere else. Gusts of uncertain wind swept past, and the proud high heads of these ancient mountains seemed contemptuous of the breathless heat far below.

McClaren debated whether he should approach Pardue's headquarters openly, or do some scouting through the canyons on either side of the ridge. He was minded to set himself to searching this vast honeycomb of tumbled upland, feeling that however long it took, the results would be the key to something.

But when he spotted a lone horseman below him to the west, riding in a wary, alert way, rifle cradled in his arms, and shortly afterward met another rider who was obviously on the lookout for trouble, his mind was made up for him. The second horseman blocked his way, curtly asking his business on Circle P.

Amiably, McClaren answered that he was on his way to Las Cruces, riding the chuck line.

"Is there a ranch hereabouts a man might get a

meal?" he asked, wondering if he sounded simple-minded. And maybe that wasn't such a bad idea.

The cowboy hesitated, but finally nodded to the southwest. "Ride on down to Circle-P headquarters. Mr. Pardue don't turn nobody away, long as a man don't aim on puttin' down roots."

Jess blinked and grinned. "All I want is to get my teeth into a half-cooked slab of steak." He rode on, conscious of hard eyes on his back.

The encounter gave him something to think about. Something smelled odd about these well-armed riders patrolling the trails. A man was generally free to ride where he pleased, long as he minded his own business. And it was standard to feed any man passing through, without question.

Maybe Toland's hint had something to it. Jess nudged Capitan on at a trot.

He halted the horse at last on the trail near the ranchyard. The cook was banging a pan at the cookshack door, and the tinny sound rose in the still, hot air.

He studied the layout. The house was nothing much to brag on, perhaps because Pardue was a bachelor. The barns and corrals were in good shape. There were plenty of good horses both in the corrals and in the pastures nearby.

In the rush to dinner by the hands, McClaren counted four men. He rode down after they were inside the cookshack. Two other men were approaching as Capitan dainty-stepped into sight near the corrals.

The two walking to the shack stopped short, obviously startled to see a stranger. McClaren rode up easy-like, reined in and relaxed in the saddle, pushing his hat back.

"Howdy. Could a man get a meal here?" he inquired, studying the two men. Nothing much remarkable about either of them. One was a dried-up old cowman. The other was younger, an ordinary puncher, his face sun-browned under black hair that seeped out from under the sweat band of his hat.

It was only their reaction to McClaren's sudden appearance that seemed unusual. The cowboy gave a quick glance toward the cookshack and then back at McClaren, who thought the man looked just plain scared.

"Git down, mister," said the older man, somewhat reluctantly. "I reckon there's enough grub to go around." He gave his companion a tiny nod. Like a shot the other left them and hurried away to the cookshack.

Jess tied the bay to the hitch rail. "Much obliged. This the Circle P?"

"It is. I'm Calvin Pardue."

McClaren shook the rancher's hand, which was thin and mottled with age spots. Pardue scrutinized Jess narrowly.

"My name's McClaren."

"McClaren!" The cowman stared. "You the feller staying over to the J-bar-W?"

Jess nodded. "I'm surprised you've heard about me."

"You pack a reputation, son," Pardue said. "I heard you and Pete Gabaldon tangled over in the Jornada. You rode out. He didn't. That ke-rect?"

Now how in the world had that word reached this isolated ranch? Jess felt a scratch of caution along his spine. "There's always some kind of gossip blowin' around," he said.

Pardue glanced again toward the building where his hands were eating. "You are a cool one," he muttered.

"No sir. Just a hungry drifter," Jess said pointedly, starting toward the steps. What was in there that Mr. Pardue was so nervous of?

Pardue grasped Jess's elbow lightly, halting him. It confirmed Jess's suspicions that the rancher wanted to keep him out of the cookshack as long as possible. And he must have an urgent reason to delay Jess, otherwise he'd never have risked laying a hand on an armed stranger.

McClaren's eyes narrowed and hardened on the older man. Hastily Pardue released his arm.

"How is Joe Ed Whitley?" Pardue said hastily. "I been hearing he's plumb sick."

"He's some better. Or he was until last night."

McClaren watched Pardue intently. "We had ourselves a little disturbance over to the J-bar-W."

"That so?"

"Somebody broke into the house, came into Whitley's room. It's a wonder he didn't get his fool head blown off. Joe Ed ain't too weak to lift the gun he keeps by him."

Pardue frowned and pursed his lips. McClaren thought something he had said had surprised and worried the old rancher. But it wasn't the fact that there'd been a ruckus at Whitley's. Had Pardue already known about that?

"In Joe Ed's room you say?" he asked now.

Jess nodded. "Bending over his bed, Mr. Whitley says. A shock for a sick old man with a bad heart."

"What's the world coming to?" Pardue mumbled. "A man ain't safe in his own bed."

Jess nodded. "Ain't it the truth? Now do you think we could go in and eat before those hands of yours go through all the grub?"

There was no further excuse for Pardue to delay. He led Jess into the cookshack.

Odd how silent the room was. The men applied themselves to their plates, eyes down, except for a few quick sideways glances as Jess came in.

Casually Jess stepped to the side of the open door, stood with the warped pine-plank wall behind him as he looked over the men at the long table.

Nothing was there to smell of menace. All the hands were busily forking meat and beans into their mouths, not even talking among themselves.

Only one fact stood out. There should have been five punchers feeding their faces, counting the one who had walked down with Pardue. There were only four. Where was the missing man?

Pardue indicated a place at table. Pointedly, not caring what conjectures his move might raise, McClaren picked his own spot, keeping his back to a windowless wall.

Somebody handed McClaren a large bowl of stew. "You're just in time," the puncher said. "Willy here ain't had his seconds yet."

"Reckon I don't eat as fast as you, Benson," came the expected retort. "Here, stranger, have some beans."

The men began to talk, and McClaren knew that the moment the men had half-feared, perhaps half-hoped for, had passed. Some crisis had been averted. He knew it for sure when he heard a horse somewhere nearby leaving at a hard run. Odd, one of the hands must suddenly have lost his appetite, and was riding out. Seemed to be headed east, upcanyon, on the trail Jess had come in on.

McClaren ate, gave his host a courteous thank-you, and went to his horse with the general exodus of the crew. To a man they clustered admiringly around the bay stud.

"Say, mister, this is some hoss! Wanta sell him? I'll give you a year's wages!" the man called Willy exclaimed. He was a sawed-off, broad-faced little man with the bowed legs and slim hips of a lifetime horseman.

"Hell"—another rider spat on the ground—"that wouldn't buy the left hind hoof of this stud."

"Where'd you git him?" Willy asked, then gave Jess a nervous look. The question wasn't the wisest.

McClaren grinned. "Didn't steal him, if that's what you're thinking."

"Will you sell him?" Willy persisted, his heart in his eyes.

"No, but you can try him out if you want. Take it easy on the bit—you cut his mouth and I'll feed you to him."

"No sir! I'll handle him as delicate as if I was a New York City lady out for a ride in the park," Willy swore, much to the hilarity of his friends.

The short man untied the bay, swung lightly into the saddle, and turned him away from the crowd of punchers, who watched with interest. With these men, nothing was much more appealing than a good horse. McClaren felt at home with them, in spite of his conviction that something ugly was being hidden here.

Willy nudged the stud into his silken-footed canter, loping a short distance toward the upper canyon. He had just started to turn the stallion around when something made his head jerk back, eyes widened in surprise. It was only then the men heard the report of a rifle from somewhere up on the ridge.

Slowly, as if reluctant to accept his death, Willy fell forward and slid off the bay. The cowboy's neck was a mass of blood when the men reached him, his eyes blankly turned up to the cloudless sky.

Cursing low and steady, McClaren caught the bay and then collared one of the punchers bending over their fallen comrade.

"Who was that?" he gritted. "Who fired that shot?"

The man's face was greenish white. "I don't know, mister. Lemme go!"

"You'll tell me or I'll—" McClaren dropped Capitan's reins and his gun was in his hand, the movement a half-seen blur.

"No sir! I cain't tell you!" gasped the cowboy.

Pardue entered the group, his face like gray chalk, his mouth a thin grim line.

"Let Bob go, McClaren. I'll tell you what you want to know. Come on up the house where we can talk."

"I believe I've lost my taste for your hospitality, Pardue," Jess said. "You'll get on a horse and ride out of here with me."

The cowman hesitated, then nodded, and with a glance at the eastern ridges brooding in the midday heat, he gestured to one of his men. "Bring me my horse."

"We'd best stand here in the group, McClaren," he said calmly, "until I've got my mount. He thinks maybe he got you, but could be he won't rest until he's sure. When you get on that bay, you better make him fly if you want to stay alive. I'll keep up as best I can. Take the road down the canyon."

McClaren sensed that Pardue was sincere, as shaken by what had happened here as any of the men. His jaw was clenched under skin paled with anger, his mouth a thin line. Yes, Pardue had crossed some line in his mind with the senseless killing of his hired hand. A code had been violated, and minds were being changed fast, here. So could Jess trust the rancher now?

Jess had known men like Calvin Pardue all his life. He'd kill without hesitation if he believed it was rightful. But he wouldn't lie to lead an innocent man into a trap.

"I'd rather go after that bushwhacker," Jess said. Pardue nodded, eyes clear and steady as a young man's.

"Wellsir, so would I. But it sure could be he's got the drop on us, and there ain't no way he'd miss with you in his sights all the way to the ridge crest. You'd best do it my way, today."

"You didn't expect this?" Jess asked, already knowing the answer in the old rancher's bleak look.

"Reckon you'll form your own opinion about that, McClaren. If the words of an old man's any use to you, before God almighty, I didn't."

The cowboy brought Pardue's horse. "All right, Mr. Pardue," Jess said. "Get on."

When the rancher was mounted, Jess leaped into his own saddle. He let out a yell that set Capitan's black-tipped ears flat of his head, and his hooves scrambling, scattering cowboys. The man and horse moved like something fired from a cannon.

Wind whipped past McClaren's face as he bent low in the saddle. No need to spur the tall stud. The bay loved nothing better than a flat-out run, and the pounding hooves of Pardue's dun behind was incentive enough to keep the stallion moving like a streak of blood-red lightning.

There was another shot, a distant, dull boom. The bullet came nowhere near. The next one did, whistling past Jess's bent shoulders with the vicious whine of a maddened hornet. Real good shot, the killer. McClaren's gut tightened.

A half-dozen more jumps and they were out of range and safely into the tunnel of trees over the wagon road that led west.

A half mile further on, Jess judged it safe to stop. He pulled the sweating stud to a stop. Capitan reared with excitement, dancing, pulling at the bit. McClaren patted his sweat-shining neck.

"Hold it, old buddy. We gotta wait for somebody."

In a few seconds the hard-driven dun cowpony came into sight and was yanked to a halt by Pardue's experienced hands.

Jess knew a quick respect for the man.

"I reckon he'll be racing along that ridge, about there," Pardue said, pointing north to the canyon rim. "He's riding a good horse, and there's a purty good trail up there. He'll expect to see us come out about a mile below here, down in that meadow. Unless I miss my guess, he'll be there waiting for us, because the way the canyon winds we got further to go."

"What's your suggestion?" Jess asked.

"We climb out behind him. We might could slip past and back toward J-bar-W without he sees us."

"Mr. Pardue," Jess said with cool menace. "I want that buzzard. If we can top the ridge behind him, we can come down on him from a direction he don't expect."

Pardue grunted and led the way up the mountain slope.

They found a gully, a dry stream bed that doubtless carried rushing water in a thunderstorm, but now was knee-deep in last year's oak leaves, from the brush that densely cloaked the mountainside.

There was small chance they'd be spotted here, but the footing was bad, the draw strewn with boulders of all sizes, hidden under the softly rustling layers of old leaves.

The horses moved slowly, straining over steep places where the gully floor formed ledges one and two feet high. To save Capitan's strength for later, Jess got down and led the bay. Pardue followed his example.

At last they stood at the top of the ridge, breaking into the open after a cautious pause to look and listen.

There were no sounds of their quarry. McClaren handed the bay's reins to his companion and began to cut for sign along the ridge trail.

McClaren was quickly satisfied that the bushwhacker had passed this way, probably not many minutes past. The dusty trail displayed deep-cut hoof marks of a running horse. He signaled to the rancher, who brought the horses along.

"I'm going after him, Pardue," Jess said, adjusting a stirrup. "I ain't asking for your company, but I want you to tell me who I'm trailing, and what the devil he's got against me."

There was no answer. McClaren turned his head impatiently, to find himself staring into the muzzle of a much-used Peacemaker.

"Sorry, son, but I cain't let you go after him just yet," the old man announced. "All in good time."

Jess's lips tightened. "I believed you, Mr. Pardue. You gave me your word."

"I only said I didn't expect no cold-blooded killin' back there, nor did I. An' I ain't trying to protect that skunk, even if it might appear I am."

"What's the idea then?"

"I got something to do first before I let you and my own men go after him. That's all I can say. Git mounted—just give me your handgun first, if you please. Ride ahead of me. And don't you lay a hand on that thirty-thirty or you won't have a hand to shoot with. I hope you believe I am serious, son."

Jess met the old man's eyes for a long tense moment, then obeyed.

Pardue sighed, a tired sound. He stuck Jess's Colt in his belt. "You'll have it back right soon. Now let's ride."

The two horsemen moved at good speed across the next canyon, up the ridge to the crest, and from there the twenty-odd miles to J-bar-W. Mr. Pardue was not inclined to conversation. He seemed much absorbed by his own dark thoughts. Not that it made him less alert to his captive. All Jess had to do was shift in his saddle and glance sideways back at Pardue to see the muzzle of the Peacemaker lifting in a businesslike gesture.

Grimly McClaren set the bay to a faster pace, only to provoke a quiet remark from Pardue.

"I know well you could outrun me on that dandy bay stud, McClaren, but you won't go far with a couple of holes 'twixt your shoulder blades."

Frustrated, Jess restrained the eager stallion to a speed that matched the choppy trot of Pardue's gelding.

It was nearing nightfall when they came down the trail from the crest into J-bar-W ranch headquarters. Joey came galloping to meet them on his pony. Pardue put his gun away with a glance at Jess to warn him not to take advantage.

Jess had no such intention. He was minded to see what the old rancher's purpose might be in coming here. He sat at ease in the saddle, talking to the little boy. Joey eagerly related that he had roped his first calf today and had fallen off his horse in doing so, but had gotten back on again. And Maggie had scolded and told him to be more careful, so he had found another bunch of cows up the canyon and chased the calves all afternoon.

McClaren glanced at the tired and sweated pony the child rode and was prepared to believe Joey had done exactly what he said.

"Catch another one?" he asked soberly.

"No sir, but I'll git me one tomorrow, you wait and see," Joey promised.

"Sure you will, son." They came alongside of the corrals. McClaren got down, giving Capitan's reins to Joey. "Ask one of the men to unsaddle him for me, Joey. I'll be out to tend to him in a little while."

"I'll feed him, Jess," the boy offered eagerly. "I'll rub him down too."

"Watch he don't kick you, and don't give him too much grain." Jess slapped the bay's rump as Joey led him away.

Pardue stayed mounted, following Jess up to the house, where lamps glowed in the windows.

"All right, stop a minute, McClaren," he muttered.

Jess obeyed, turning.

"Now then. Is Joe Ed able to be out o' bed?" Pardue asked.

"He was, last I knew."

"Then step in an' tell him a old friend is out here and would like a word with him. I trust you to do as I ask. I think you'll see later why I have to ask it."

McClaren nodded and stepped into the house by the back door.

Chapter Twelve

The kitchen was warm, fragrant with the cinnamon smell of apple pie. At the table George Owens sat drinking coffee. Manuela was rolling tortillas with the slender rolling pin she used.

Owens grinned at McClaren. "Say there, Mr. McClaren, I been wanting to see you and thank you for sending me here."

Jess nodded and reached to shake hands. "You're the one needs thanking, Mr. Owens. I took your advice."

"Heard about that," Owens said, sobering. "I'm right glad you made it out of that snake's den."

"Amen, brother! Have you seen Mr. Whitley?"

"I believe he is resting in his room."

"See you later, Owens." McClaren strode across the kitchen and into the hallway leading to Joe Ed's room. He met Maggie in the dim corridor, her arms full of laundry, fresh off the line. Jess frowned at the thought of Maggie having to work so late.

"Jess!" she cried gladly at sight of him. "I've been so worried. No one knew where you'd gone."

"Sorry, Maggie. I had an errand." He read the anxiety in her eyes and something turned over in his chest. He took her face between his hands, feeling that his fingers were too hard and clumsy to touch her skin and the silken thickness of her coiled hair. With his thumb he gently traced the delicate hollow of her temple and bent to kiss her cheek.

"Jess!" she protested with a smothered laugh. "Someone will see."

"I don't care," he said gruffly, but he stepped back. "Maggie, I need to talk to Joe Ed."

"He's sleeping, I think."

"It's important."

She nodded, stepped aside to let him pass.

Whitley was snoring softly, but he came awake instantly when McClaren touched his shoulder.

"What is it?" he asked sharply. "Oh, it's you, son. Where you been?"

"Over to Pardue's place. He came back with me. Wants to talk to you."

"Bring him in then!" Whitley said testily.

McClaren shrugged. "He was set on waiting outside. By the way, he brought me here at the point of a gun. Maybe he'll explain that to you."

Joe Ed got up slowly, pulled on his boots.

"Held a gun on you, huh? I cain't hardly believe he'd do that. We been friends for years."

"Someone at Circle P tried to bushwhack me, got one of Pardue's hands instead. Pardue got the drop on me to keep me from trailing the killer."

Whitley stared at him for a moment. "Where is Cal?" he asked grimly.

"Out back. Wants to talk with you private."

It was an hour later that Jess, down at the stables, saw Joe Ed go back into the house after sitting on a stump near the woodpile listening to Cal Pardue Whitley's steps were unsteady, his shoulders slumped. Pardue wheeled his horse to trot over to where McClaren stood.

"Mr. Pardue, what the hell is this all about?" Jess asked.

"You got time for a palaver?"

"Sure."

"Let's go someplace we won't be heard."

"No secrets around here," Jess said.

Pardue glanced at Curly Brissom and José, leaning up against the fence, heads turned curiously in their direction. Red Warner was seated by the bunkhouse wall, smoking.

"What I got to say is for your ears, not theirs," Pardue said. "I had to get Joe Ed's say-so before talking even to you."

Puzzled, McClaren climbed over the fence and went with Pardue a short distance from the corrals. "Now then. What did you want to say?"

"That feller that shot Willy, thinking he was you. He come on my place about two months or more ago. I'm sorry to tell you I made him welcome. I wish to God I had run him off at the point of a rifle."

"Who is he?"

Pardue hesitated, glancing down toward the ranch house, standing secure and welcoming with its windows alight.

"I thought he'd been bad-treated," he muttered. "Told me he needed a place to bunk. I saw no harm in it. Said he'd been lied about by Miss Bourne—"

McClaren's head lifted sharply. "What about Miss Bourne?"

The older man's mouth worked uneasily. "All them years ago, when the girl got herself in trouble, after Joe Ed took her in and raised her, provided every bite she had to eat, then he run off his own son on account of her."

"You got that story a little mixed up, mister!" Jess snapped. "Whitley's son made Maggie believe they were married. Staged a fake ceremony. He used her a way no decent man would use a woman, good or bad, and then deserted her. Joe Ed found her half-dead, out on the desert. Now do you blame Whitley for kicking his boy out?"

Pardue shook his head. "Hell, son. I never knew all that, and when Daniel turned up looking like he'd been through hell, I felt right sorry for him. I'd knew that boy all his life."

"You're saying it's Joe Ed's son that had me in his sights up on that ridge today, who killed your puncher?"

"That's right, McClaren. That's why I couldn't let you follow his trail, maybe kill him. I owed something to his daddy."

"You've told all this to Whitley?"

"I have. He has a right to know. Now I can go back with a clean conscience and set the law onto that cowardly backshooter." Pardue's voice trembled, but it was from a consuming fury, not weakness.

"Why is Daniel Whitley gunning for me?"

"That I cain't say. He said men were out to kill him—talked me into sending out riders to check strangers. Well, hell, I got more than one boy punchin' cows fer me who's got no love for the law."

He turned, climbed into his saddle. "I'll be riding now."

"I'll come with you."

"Do no good. Daniel will have cleared out by now, nor would he even come back fer his bedroll if he knows what's good fer him. I got no fast-draw artists in my crew, but ain't a one of my men would hesitate to shoot down a stinkin', bushwackin' buzzard if he shows hisself. Them fellers thought a lot of Willy. My men will be combing the canyons for his murderer."

With a nod, the old cowman touched spurs to his pony and loped away up the canyon.

McClaren stood staring thoughtfully after him. What did it all mean? Joe Ed's son breaking into the house last night, bending over his father in the darkness, then today putting a coward's bullet into the rider he took to be McClaren?

According to Pardue, he'd been living at Circle P for months. Why was he lingering in these parts?

Jess frowned. There was still so damned much he didn't understand!

There was a footstep behind him. Jess whirled, automatically drawing his Colt.

"Easy man!" Warner laughed. "It's me."

"Sorry." Jess straightened, replacing the gun.

"A mite jumpy, ain't you? What was ol' man Pardue looking so down-dog about?"

Briefly, Jess recounted the day's happenings.

Warner's face was uncharacteristically still. "You telling me Joe Ed's boy lit out when you rode onto the place, then tried to kill you? I don't believe it!"

"It's true," Jess said. "Daniel was the man in the house last night."

"You don't say!" Warner turned abruptly away, starting down the trail slowly, head bent in thought.

"What would he be doing, creepin' into his old home like a damned thief?" McClaren asked.

Abruptly Red shrugged. "Blamed if I know. Let's go in to supper."

The other hands and Joey already were digging into the hot food. Jess tossed his hat on a peg and sat down beside the boy. Maggie was slicing bread. She glanced at him, eyes alight.

George Owens came in, diffidently, as if still not sure of his welcome.

"Sit and eat, Owens," Red invited. "Guess you've found out there ain't anything as good as Manuela's steak."

Owens had evidently been at pains to improve his appearance. His shirt was patched, but clean, his face well scrubbed, as were his hands, up to his wrists. "Say, I found where a mountain lion got a good young heifer, over to Apache Canyon. Think I'll ride over there an' camp tonight. See can I get a shot at that ol' cat."

Manuela placed a cup of steaming coffee before the puncher. Warner handed him the meat platter.

"Mr. Owens," Joey demanded. "Tell that story you told me, about the time you was hunting deer in the winter and the mountain lion came down on you and your horse and you—"

Maggie squelched her son. "Let Mr. Owens tell the story, Joey."

"Wellsir," began Owens, "it was in seventy-five, up in Montana—"

He seemed to gain confidence as he got into his tale, half of which was probably pure invention, but entertaining nevertheless. When Owens finished the story, Curly thought of one, some long-winded saga of a time he rode unwittingly into an area around a rattlesnake den and got himself thrown from his horse.

Jess listened with half his attention, mulling over the problem of Daniel Whitley.

Refusing a second slice of pie, he rose from the table and went to find Joe Ed.

Whitley was in his room, sitting in the dark by a window, head in his hands.

"Mind if I come in?" Jess asked from the doorway.

"Huh? Oh, sure son. Just light that lamp there, if you want."

Jess did so, and shut the door. He studied Whitley. The man appeared to have aged in the last hour. McClaren waited for the old cowman to speak, wondering what must be going through the man's mind.

"He wasn't never any good," Joe Ed said at last. "His ma and me spoiled him. But we never made him into a backshooter."

"No sir." Jess wished he had words to comfort him. "Sometimes a man just goes wrong on his own."

"I been an honest man, overall." Whitley leaned tiredly back in his old, high-backed rocker. "I never asked for what I didn't earn. I've killed men, but never one that didn't need killin'. An' never from the back, without warning."

"I believe you, Mr. Whitley."

The old man's voice was rusty. "I saw the bad in my son, but I thought it was just weakness for a pretty girl, like most boys. I run him off for what he done to Maggie. Maybe I was wrong to send him away."

Remembering Maggie's fear and disgust of the younger Whitley, Jess shook his head. "You did the only thing you could, to protect Maggie."

The older man sighed. "That was my thinking. But I didn't know, when I kicked Danny out, that Maggie was carrying his son. I would have made him marry her proper."

"She wouldn't have done it," Jess said.

"I believe you're right. In that one night, she learned to despise the boy she'd loved all her life."

"All that's past and done," Jess reminded quietly.

"Reckon that's true. It ain't no use to think about what fork in the road might have been better to travel. All a man can do is go on. But what I'm thinking now is, what will it do to Maggie and to Joey when my boy is caught and hanged?"

"He might not be caught. Many a man is running free with as bad on his conscience."

That seemed to relieve Whitley a little. He looked at Jess with a glimmering of hope. "Wellsir, that's right. He might head for the border now, and stay out o' sight. McClaren, I'm a old fool, I know that, but I cain't hardly bear to think of my only boy with a noose around his neck! I'd druther he was shot clean and quick, than that." The rancher's veined hands clenched.

McClaren stood. "Why don't you get some rest? None of this was your doing, and you can't do anything about any of it right now."

"Mrs. Whitley hated me for running our boy off," Joe Ed said softly, as if he had not heard Jess. "She said she wisht she'd took him and lived with her brother, down to Roswell, when I brought Maggie into the house. She hated me for that, and for takin' up for the girl against our son. I—I reckon she took her revenge the only way she could, making up to every man who crossed her path, till I made her stay to home, behave herself."

He ran big hands that trembled over his hollowed cheeks. "God! If a man could just only go back to when he was young and had the control o' things, and do different."

Jess felt troubled, unwilling to hear more of this good man's secret torments. Tomorrow he would be sorry he had bared his sorrows to a near-stranger. "I reckon every man wishes that sometimes," he said gently. "Now, you need to get some rest. Good night, Mr. Whitley."

Jess went to his own room, feeling last night's lack of sleep. He lay down without removing his boots. The dark room was quiet. Jess fastened his mind once more on the things that had been happening on J-bar-W and Pardue's spread.

For hours, urgent thoughts pushing fatigue back, he lay thinking. At last he thought he had answers to some of the questions. But they only turned themselves over to present more, and harder, problems.

Sighing, he rolled himself up in the blankets and was asleep almost at once.

Chapter Thirteen

Morning brought a new problem. Red Warner did not show up at breakfast. Curly Brissom reported that Red had not slept in his bunk last night.

Leaving his own breakfast untouched, Jess went to the bunkhouse with Curly. They looked over Red's meager possessions. The extra shirt, tin of tobacco, pair of old boots in need of half soling, and a couple of pair of faded pants told them nothing. Nothing of significance seemed to be missing.

"He didn't come in until late last night, but I didn't think nothing about it," Curly said. "I heard him, but I didn't really wake up. I guess he must've gone right back out again, an' I never knew it."

"Where is George Owens?"

"He's huntin' that cougar."

Jess nodded. "Yeah, I'd forgotten." He left the bunkhouse and headed for the corral.

The horses had already been fed—Curly always attended to that before breakfast. Jess looked for the horse Warner most often rode, a chunky black steeldust that was Red's own property—and probably the most valuable item the cowboy owned. The gelding was gone, as were Warner's saddle, chaps, and other gear.

McClaren stood in the hot sunlight, thinking. Two questions came to mind. The first, of course, was where Warner had gone in the middle of the night. The second, did he go of his free will, or did somebody force him to go?

For twenty minutes Jess examined tracks in the corral area. Joe Ed, coming to the barns for the first time since his illness, found him there. The older man took off his ancient Stetson and rubbed away the sweat of unaccustomed exertion with his shirtsleeve.

"Was Red made to ride out?" he asked bluntly.

Jess shook his head. "I can't tell much from the tracks. Too many of 'em. I'll see if I can cut his trail."

He lifted his lariat off his saddle in the shed and headed for the corral where Capitan was lapping up the last of his oats.

Whitley called him back. "Wait, son. You ain't et. Go on up to the house and have breakfast before you ride."

"I'd like to get onto Warner's tracks as soon as I can."

"A few more minutes cain't hurt. I'll send Curly out to look for Red too. Thataway you won't have to cover so much ground."

Jess went back to the house with the old man, slowing his long strides to let Joe Ed keep up. Even so, Whitley was breathing hard by the time they climbed the back steps.

"No sign of him?" Maggie asked.

McClaren shook his head.

"It isn't like Red to go off without saying anything." Maggie frowned.

"What do *you* know about it?" came an unexpected voice. It was Mrs. Whitley, appearing in the doorway.

Anna was looking less attractive than usual this morning. Her face was colorless and the lines showed up harshly about her eyes, as if she hadn't slept. Jess wondered if she'd heard the talk about her son murdering Pardue's man, mistaking him for McClaren.

Apparently she had, for her next bitter remark was directed to Jess.

"I suppose you sent Red out to track down my boy like an animal!"

"Anna, we'll have no more such talk!" barked her husband.

The blond woman turned on him, her lips flattened over her teeth. "Don't say a word to me, old man, not one word! It was you drove Danny away from his own home, on the say-so of that slut. You love her and her bastard more than your own flesh and blood. It was you drove my son to dangerous acts, it was you! And his blood will be on your hands if—"

Joe Ed had seated himself at the table. Now he rose unsteadily, his big-nosed face stern and cold. "Woman!" he thundered. "You take your vicious tongue out o' here, or I'll see that you do. This is still my house. I won't—I won't—"

He caught a hard breath and clutched at his chest, bending double. "Maggie!" he gasped.

McClaren leaped to catch him as he slumped.

"Dear God, it's his heart," Maggie cried. "Help me get him to his room."

"*Madre de Dios!*" cried Manuela.

McClaren picked up Joe Ed's frail form, shouldered Anna Whitley aside, and carried the old man to his bed. Joe Ed's face was gray, with a blue tinge under the skin. He struggled for each breath. McClaren laid him down, and turned. Anna hovered in the doorway, wide-eyed, hand over her mouth. Jess hoped savagely that she fully realized what she had done to her husband with her wild accusations.

"Where can I find a doctor?" he demanded.

Maggie was loosening Whitley's collar, removing the bandanna from around his neck. Her dark eyes were tear-filled. "Tularosa. Dr. Potter. His home is near the general store."

McClaren ran from the house. In moments he'd caught the bay stud and was throwing the saddle on. Curly came panting up beside him. "Want me to go for the doc, McClaren?"

"No. See if you can track Warner. Take José. Ask Concepcion to stay near the house in case Maggie needs help with Mr. Whitley."

McClaren mounted. He did not wait for Curly to open the corral gate, but sent the stud over it as lightly as a swallow. Capitan landed running, his long legs devouring ground.

*   *   *

Jess reined in before leaving the foothills to let the bay rest. There was a windmill and tank about a mile down into the flats, he recalled. He could water the horse there, but he'd have to cool him first. He kept the horse to a walk as they left the hills and descended into the hot, sun-seared basin, where hummocky red sand supported tangled growths of stubborn mesquite and greasewood. The land lay still as death.

Heat waves lifted, shimmering over the distant lava beds and to the southwest, above the white-hot Sands.

At the windmill, McClaren's horse edged aside a bunch of thin, thirsty cattle and put his head down to sniff at the inch or so of scummy water in the tank. The stream of water the mill usually produced had vanished in the absence of wind. From the look of the supply, it couldn't be more than a finger's width of flow, at best.

McClaren sighed, dismounted, and loosened the cinch while the bay drank. He pulled the horse away from the water before Capitan was satisfied. Filling up with water would only slow the bay in the grueling race ahead.

McClaren tightened the cinch and mounted. He urged the stud into a long trot, ignoring the wagon road and taking the most direct route toward Tularosa. It would mean rougher terrain and deep gullies to cross, but might save a few precious minutes of Joe Ed's time.

The hours went sluggishly by as the bay horse with the tall rider moved through the blow sand and scrubby brush. A roadrunner leaped into view, gliding swiftly away into the security of the desert.

Again McClaren rested his horse a scant few minutes, then pushed hard toward the distant town.

Heat and thirst beat at him. He ignored the discomfort, intent on putting miles behind him, grateful for the toughness of the thoroughbred, knowing Capitan would go until he dropped.

Only when the town was in view some two miles away and they came out on the better footing of the wagon road did McClaren touch the stud with spurs and let him lengthen his deep-chested body into a run.

To have done so before would have burned the big horse out, and maybe left McClaren afoot in the desert.

Now the bay proved he still had the power to do the job at hand, in spite of the wearying forty miles of travel through hoof-clinging sand. Willingly he leaped into a run, neck thrust forward, ears laid back. His neck dripped sweat. Foam edged his mouth.

Grimly McClaren bent low over the horse's mane but he did not spur or whip him. It was unnecessary.

Red dust flew behind them as they raced into Tularosa. McClaren looked for the general store, and next to it the home of the town's only doctor. It was a small adobe house next to an *acequia* where giant cottonwoods leaned, shading the hard-beaten ground and the dry irrigation ditch.

McClaren leaped off the bay before the animal halted. He left him ground-tied and ran for the door of the doctor's house, pounding on it with a hard fist.

A small, round, Mexican woman obeyed his summons, peering at him with wide eyes. The doctor's wife explained that the doctor was attending an injured farmer north of town. The man had cut his foot with an ax. She called her son to take a message to Dr. Potter. The boy untied a horse that stood saddled at the hitch rail. Whipping and kicking at its sides with bare heels, he lit out along the street. McClaren was relieved to see that the boy rode as well as an Indian and the mustang was wiry and fast.

McClaren led his horse down the street to a livery stable. A very fat man roused from his siesta and looked at the newcomer querulously.

"Don't disturb yourself, *amigo,*" McClaren told him. "I'll rub him down myself and feed him. How much for oats and hay?"

The stableman named a sum. McClaren tossed him the coins and led the bay into the shady, fly-humming stable.

The stud seemed little the worse for wear after his hard ride, but Jess left nothing to chance. He rubbed the stud down well, massaging knotted muscles in shoulder and foreleg. When Capitan was cool, he let him drink, then gave him a sparing feed of oats and plenty of good hay. When he was sure the horse was comfortable, he awarded himself a long, cool drink from the pump. He poked a boot toe gently in the side of the snoring gentleman in charge of the stable.

The man snorted and heaved himself up in alarm. "*Que pasa?*"

"I want to rent a good horse. I'll leave mine here, be back for him as soon as I can. You give him the best of care, you hear?" Jess handed him ten dollars. "Anything happens to that horse, I'll take it out of your skin. *comprende,* hombre?"

Nervously, the Mexican assured him that he understood "*muy bueno!*"

McClaren roped a tough, well-muscled dun from the several mounts available in the corral. He saddled quickly and headed out of town.

In late afternoon he intercepted the doctor's buggy, in the foothills leading into Venado Canyon.

The doctor's fat sorrel mare was trotting amiably along, responding to the doctor's cluckings with the flick of an ear, but not much speed. The doctor looked up as Jess rode alongside.

"You the fellow sent the message about Mr. Whitley?"

"Yes sir. Can't you get up a little more steam there, Doc? Mr. Whitley needs you now, not next week."

"I'm doin' my best," snapped the medical man, brandishing his buggy whip but not striking the complacent mare. "Say, ain't you the man I treated awhile back? McClaren?"

"That's right. Stop your Sunday school pony. I'll put this dun in the shafts."

"Are you crazy, man?" Doc Potter pulled his mare to a halt, something that required no coaxing at all. "That horse has prob'ly never been worked in harness."

"No sir," McClaren agreed. "Reckon he hasn't."

He was already stripping his saddle off while the doctor nervously led his mare out of the shafts. The exchange, with the mare carrying Jess's saddle and the dun harnessed, took only a few minutes. The dun, fractious by nature, rolled a white-rimmed eye. He was controlled, barely, by the doctor's uncertain hands on the reins until Jess could jump aboard.

McClaren took the lines and shook them out. He reached for the whip. "Better get a grip, Doc," he suggested, and gave the dun a sharp tap on the rump.

The horse stared back at them over his shoulder, dumbfounded by the contraption crowding his rear. McClaren gave him another tap, and the situation exploded. The dun tried to leap skyward, encountered the whiplash again, lunged forward instead. Fortunately he contented himself with a hard run before he wrecked the buggy. Thereafter McClaren kept him moving too fast to try anything else, using the whip with a light, persuasive touch.

The buggy mare, tied to the rear, found herself dragged along involuntarily. She tried hanging back on her rope, to no avail. Being a sensible mare, she soon resigned herself to moving fast enough to keep from being dragged, stiff-legged. Likely she hadn't put on so much speed since she was a colt.

Doc Potter sat wild-eyed, hanging on with white-knuckled hands as they bumped and lurched over ruts and rocks. His hat blew off. He hardly seemed to notice it.

The dun was a trifle hard to guide. Several times he left the road and lit out cross-country. It required all Jess's strength to turn him back in a wide, bouncing circle to the ranch road.

Their progress up the canyon was an unforgettable experience, but they were in the ranch yard before dark. The dun gelding, finally worn out by his long, uphill race, was as docile as Joey's pony when they came to a stop.

Jess expected a tongue lashing from the doctor, but the man merely climbed out of the buggy, fished a pocket flask out of a pocket, and took a great swallow of whiskey. Then he grasped his black bag and staggered toward the house. McClaren drove to the barn to tend the lathered horses. George Owens came to help him. "Damn boy, you must've flew!"

"How's Mr. Whitley?" Jess lifted the harness from the dun and handed it to Owens to hang on a fence rail.

Warren shook his head. "He ain't so good. Miss

Maggie says he ain't woke up yet. Oh, lordy," the old cowboy burst out. "Looks like I only got here in time to bury my old friend."

"Take it easy, Mr. Owens," Jess said. "Joe Ed's come through this kind of trouble before. He's got a lot of try. He won't go under without a fight."

Jess fed the horses. "Any word about Warner?"

"No sir, when I come in from Apache Canyon, I heard that he'd went off in the night. Nobody knowed any more'n that."

"Curly back yet?"

"Yeah. Said he lost Red's trail somewhere north of here."

"I better talk to him. He in the bunkhouse?"

"Was, last I knew," grunted Owens.

McClaren went to find Curly.

The cowboy was hunched over a deck of cards, alone in the bunkhouse. He looked up, expression suddenly wary, when Jess stepped in.

"What did you find?" McClaren asked without preliminaries.

"Not a danged thing. Wore my tail off ridin'—"

"You found Warner's trail, though," Jess interrupted.

Brissom shrugged defensively. "Oh sure. Plain as day, at first."

"Was he alone when he left here?"

"I couldn't tell for sure. Well, hell, there's been a dozen horses over that trail the past week!"

"You saying you can't tell which was fresh, printed over the old ones?" Jess studied Brissom narrowly. Something not quite right here. Curly wasn't the brightest puncher he'd ever known, but he had to know tracking better than that.

"He was alone, I reckon." Curly pretended a deep interest in the hand of cards he'd dealt himself.

Abruptly McClaren knocked the cards from Curly's hand to scatter over the floor. Curly looked up, his lashless, rabitty eyes fearful. "What'd you go and do that for?" he squeaked.

McClaren felt a deep disgust. "I want answers from you, Brissom, and I got no time to fool around. Which direction did Red go?"

"I already told you," whined Curly. "Look here, Mr. McClaren, you don't need to git mad at me. I done what you said. Me and José followed his tracks north, along the ridge. We lost the trail in the rockslides at Caballo Peak."

"That's a damned lie, Curly! Unless his horse sprouted wings and took off straight up or down one of those slides, he had to come out on the far side."

"I'm tellin' you. I couldn't find his trail." His eyes shifted away from Jess's.

McClaren restrained himself from slapping Curly's silly face. The man's story made no sense at all. Why was he lying? There was something here Jess ought to be seeing—

"You never crossed the slides and looked at the trail beyond!" McClaren accused.

Curly's eyes dropped. His mouth went sulky. "Hell, McClaren, it was purty near dark. There wasn't time to go on."

"I know you were back long before dark. You must have had three hours of daylight when you left the peak. Couldn't you stand to miss a meal, Curly? Or were you too yellow to follow those tracks any further?"

Curly's mouth bunched up and slid sidewise. He wouldn't meet McClaren's eyes.

Jess bored harder. "What were you scared of, Brissom?"

"Listen, McClaren," Curly almost babbled, "two men been bushwhacked in the last few weeks. I ain't no good with a gun. I thought someone was maybe watchin' us. I figured we better get back."

"Damn it, man," Jess exploded. "Your friend Red could be lying out there dead or dying, maybe just beyond where you turned back."

Curly got a mulish look on his face. "If he's dead, what good will it do to find him? An' he ain't no real friend of mine. He was always throwing his weight around. You needn't think he's bosom buddies with you neither, McClaren. I seen some of the looks he give you, to your back! An' he ain't no saint, McClaren. If Mr. Whitley knowed how cozy ol' Red an' Miz

Whitley has been, he'd a canned him long ago, an' made me foreman!"

Jess was startled. He stared at the other man with narrowed eyes. Curly cringed as if expecting a blow. With a sound of disgust, Jess turned away but stopped by the bunkhouse door.

"Brissom, be ready to ride in an hour. If I'm not needed at the house, we're going back to those slides. Saddle some horses."

"Well now, I ain't exactly sure where I lost the tracks," Curly muttered uneasily. "We'll just be covering up Red's tracks if we go over them in the dark. A man's horse could make a misstep and fall a hunnerd, two hunnerd feet!"

Jess whirled. "What's that? You aren't sure where you lost the damned trail?"

"Well—I seen where it was headin' so I wasn't paying much attention them last ten miles—"

"Ten miles!" McClaren stared at the cowboy as if he were some new kind of louse. "You saying you maybe overrode the tracks by ten miles?"

Curly shrugged, face screwed up like a cornered rat.

Jess let his breath out slowly, longing to floor the gutless, silly jackass. "We leave at first light!" he snapped, and strode out before his instincts could get in the way of his better judgment.

Chapter Fourteen

When McClaren came into the kitchen Manuela immediately began to dish up food from the warming oven. George Owens sat at the table. He looked up bleakly.

"Any word yet?" Jess asked.

"Doctor's still in there. Miss Maggie's worried sick.

She's about wore herself out. She and Manuela set with Joe Ed all day."

"Why can't Mrs. Whitley take a turn?"

Owens raised bushy gray brows. "You think that there woman is gonna dirty her dainty hands nursin' her sick husband?"

So Owens had figured Anna out already. Jess sighed. "Where's the boy?"

"I put him to bed myself. He cried hisself to sleep." Owens rubbed a hand over a whisker-stubbled chin. "What did Brissom say?"

Jess frowned. "Nothing worth telling."

Dr. Potter came in. Jess stood. "Doc, come and have some supper. Manuela's got some good venison roast."

He brought coffee for the older man and pushed the sugar across the table to him.

"Thanks, son." The doctor narrowed his eyes sternly at Jess. "That was some ride you treated me to."

"Beg pardon, Doc. It seemed necessary. How's Mr. Whitley?"

The medical man scowled. "What the hell happened to put my patient back in bed? He was doing fine last time I examined him. This setback could be impossible to remedy."

"There—was a little ruckus."

"Is that so? Well, I'll make an educated guess. It had something to do with Mrs. Whitley, isn't that it?"

Jess shrugged. "Is Mr. Whitley awake yet?"

"Yes. He wanted to talk to you, McClaren, but I told him you were away, so he'd rest. When you see to him, don't let him get excited, even if you have to lie to him about certain matters, to keep him quiet."

"You can depend on it, Doc."

Having finished his meal, the doctor rose. "I'd best get back to town, if someone would bring my buggy—and hitch my own mare, if you please! I'll look in once more on my patient."

Jess went to harness the doctor's mare. He found Concepcion and asked him to ride the hired dun back to Tularosa, accompanying the doctor.

"When you get to town, get some food and some

sleep," Jess told the boy, handing him a couple of bills from his fast-dwindling roll. "Bring my stud back tomorrow early."

"*Gracias,* Mr. McClaren!" breathed the handsome young man.

Jess woke before dawn and went out into the kitchen. The house was still. Manuela, dozing lightly in a rocking chair near the stove, had kept the fire going and coffee hot. Blessing her kind heart, Jess quietly poured himself a cup and was drinking it when she woke.

"Señor, you are riding out?" she whispered.

He nodded.

"I put supplies out for you in case you have to make the camp."

She got out of her chair, her movements betraying fatigue. Distressed when he refused to wait for breakfast, she found cold meat, half a loaf of bread and dried apples that he and Brissom could take with them.

Curly came in, with a sullen glance at McClaren, and planted himself at the table. Manuela gave him coffee, as Jess coolly informed him that breakfast would be made on the trail.

Curly opened his mouth to argue, but the issue was settled against Jess when Maggie hurried in. "We must have the doctor again. Joe Ed is worse."

Jess turned toward the door. "I'll go."

"No, Jess, please stay. Send someone else. I may—I may need you."

She looked desperately tired, her face strained and colorless, shadowed smudges under her eyes. He longed to take her in his arms.

"Well, I reckon I can have my breakfast after all, Manuela!" Curly remarked with satisfaction.

Jess turned on him. "The hell you can! You get your lazy rump out of that chair. I'd send you for the doc, but you'd probably get hungry at noon and turn back. Put José on the fastest horse in the corrals. Tell him to find Doc Potter a better buggy horse or bring him horseback."

Sullenly, Curly ambled out. Jess longed to kick him into a trot.

In a few minutes he heard Manuela's boy ride by at a run, and he felt better. José could get more out of a horse than most men. He'd have the doctor back here as soon as humanly possible.

Maggie was turning to go back into the sickroom, a basin of water in her hands. Jess intercepted her, took the pan from her.

"You're ready to drop. That won't do Joe Ed any good. You go to bed. I'll sit with him. Manuela will help me with anything that needs doing. She'll look after Joey too, won't you, Manuela?"

Manuela heartily agreed and shooed Maggie to her room. McClaren went to Joe Ed's bedside. He set the water on a table near the bed.

The older man was mumbling, twisting in his bed. McClaren caught the sound of his own name and Maggie's. He wrung out a cloth, clumsily bathed the cold sweat off Whitley's face.

"I'm here, Mr. Whitley," he said. "You take it easy. I'll be right here with you."

Whitley's eyelids fluttered open. His eyes were sunken, but they fastened gratefully on McClaren's face. Jess drew a chair close to the bed.

The old rancher seemed comforted. His eyes closed and he lay still, his breathing labored. At last he seemed to drift into sleep.

Hours passed. The household noises were subdued. Once Jess heard Joey's voice raised querulously, and as quickly hushed. Later, apparently having escaped Manuela's watchful eye for a moment, Joey slipped into the room and came to McClaren's side. He gazed at his grandfather, sighed in an oddly adult way, and leaned gratefully into the circle of Jess's arm.

"Is Grandpa gonna die?" he whispered loudly.

McClaren hesitated. The boy was too smart to accept the ready lie. "I don't know, son. We're doin' the best we can to help him."

Joey nodded gravely. He stayed for a short time with Jess, saying nothing, then tiptoed out.

Once Mrs. Whitley glanced into the room. Jess turned his head in time to catch a look of vengeful joy in her eyes as she studied her gravely ill husband. When she felt Jess's eyes on her, she smiled at him, but it was a smile filled with venomous meaning.

"What pleases you?" Jess asked abruptly.

"Why—didn't you know?" She tossed her blond head. "My boy will be coming home soon—and this time no one will send him away. No one!" She whirled and was gone into the shadows of the hall.

Concepcion got back, with the bay stud. José was with him, but he had to report that the doctor had been unable to return to J-bar-W until later. He had been called to the bedside of a young woman in difficult childbirth. Worry clenched in Jess's chest, but he knew that Mr. Whitley would have agreed with the doctor's choice, to save a new young life rather than attend an elderly, dying patient. At noon Manuela took over the vigil, sending Jess out to eat. Not hungry, McClaren left the ranch house. The day was close and still. Thunderheads were piling up in miles-high towers to the west, pressing the heat against the parched earth. McClaren knew that cowmen across this vast country were eagerly watching those clouds, praying that rain was coming at last.

Ironically, Jess had to hope it would hold off, or there would be no chance of finding the already fading traces of Red Warner's departure.

The cowpuncher's disappearance must have had something to do with the loss of Whitley's cattle, but what?

Maybe Warner had thought of something he wanted to investigate. But why ride out without a word, without a bedroll, or food, if he planned to be gone this long?

Owens appeared at Jess's side, thin and stooped. "You're itching to try and find Warner, ain't you?"

Jess nodded. "If I don't make a move soon, we may never know where Warner went. I have a feeling it's mighty important to find him."

"You think he's dead?"

"I don't know, but I've got to find out."

"McClaren, you trust me?"

Jess turned to the aging rider with surprise.

"Why, sure—" He read the other's face and knew

instinctively he shouldn't answer without giving the question sober thought.

"Yes sir, Mr. Owens," he said, after a moment. "I believe you can be trusted."

Owens gave a satisfied nod. Jess knew he'd said what the other needed to hear, and knew also that his statement of trust could be made with confidence. Owens was of the old stamp, a breed of men who had lived hard and faced whatever life threw in their path with a kind of honor that was tough as rawhide. Their ways didn't always set well with the townspeople, nor with lawmen who didn't hold with quick and final justice. But it was a code you could bet on to stay the same.

"Well, then," Owens said briskly. "You let me take over here. I'll explain the problem to Miss Bourne, and you see can you find Warner's trail. He could be needin' help."

Jess hesitated only briefly, then nodded. He saddled a stocky black gelding. He couldn't help glancing worriedly back at the ranch house.

"Don't you fret, boy!" Owens advised. "All's being done that can be. I'll send that worthless Curly from the bunkhouse to go with you, though what good he'll be, I dunno." Owens slapped Jess's shoulder and hobbled stiffly away.

To save time, Jess saddled Brissom's usual mount, a lean *grulla* gelding with no great speed or endurance, but the easiest saddle gait of any of the ranch horses.

Curly slouched out of the bunkhouse, looking as if he'd been sound asleep. He took the *grulla*'s reins without a civil word. Shrugging, Jess swung into his saddle.

"Ain't you riding that stud of yours?" Curly asked.

"Turned him out in the horse trap. He's due a rest."

"I swear, I believe you care more about them horses than you do about yourself. If I had a horse like that there, I'd ride him, come hell or high water!"

"Sure you would," Jess drawled. "All the way up to suppertime."

As they moved out, Joey came running from the

house with a packet of food Owens had sent out. Jess reined the black in.

"Can I go with you, McClaren?" The child's eyes were begging.

"Sorry, son, not this time. You stay and take good care of your grandpa."

Looking rebellious, Joey turned away.

There was a low rumble of thunder. "We'd better ride," Jess said, and took the lead at a fast trot.

The two men rode without pause to the head of Venado Canyon. McClaren already knew Red had come this way, so there was no need as yet to study the tracks closely. He knew the print of the horse Warner had taken. Stopping where the trails forked just under the ridge, he studied the hard-packed ground to satisfy himself that Warner had turned his horse north.

The clouds were thickening now, pushing ahead of them a chill breeze that felt strange after the earlier smothering heat. Wind sprang up, whipping itself into a dust devil in the dry grass, swirling chokingly over the two riders.

The whirlwind roared like a miniature twister, beating against the men, stinging their faces with bits of gravel and twigs caught up from the ground. The black Jess rode snorted and reared. He came down straining for the bit, humped for action. Jess held him steady. The wind roared away down the eastern slopes as he spurred the horse forward, untying his slicker and shrugging into it as he rode.

Lightning cracked on the spine of the ridge ahead, followed swiftly by ground-rocking thunder.

"McClaren, we don't git off this ridge, that lightning's gonna fry us both!" Brissom's lumpy face was pale.

"We're following these tracks!" Jess said, letting his horse move out, keeping his eye on the faint hoof marks.

Brissom kept up a steady shrill of complaint about the storm, but Jess stuck doggedly to the task, and they covered a mile before the rain hit, coming at first in fat, hesitant, widely scattered drops and then in a steadily increasing rush of water, needle-sharp and achingly cold. Sleet mixed with the rain, stinging horses and men.

After a half hour of drenching downpour, Jess had to admit defeat. Their own tracks were being washed out as swiftly as the horses stepped. Warner's trail was gone now. It was useless to ride aimlessly in the storm, unable to see more than a few feet away.

Gritting his teeth with frustration, McClaren led the way down off the ridge into a canyon on the west side.

They were back at the ranch by dark, their mission a failure.

There were two buggies at the house. Water dripping off his hat brim, McClaren tended to the black gelding and put out grain and hay for Capitan, then walked to the house.

No one was in the kitchen. McClaren helped himself to hot water and went to his room to change his wet clothing. He was soaked to the skin.

As he was buttoning his shirt, Manuela tapped on his door.

"Señor McClaren, Miss Maggie heard you come in. She wishes you to come to Mr. Whitley's room."

Whitley's room seemed crowded. McClaren hesitated near the door. Maggie came at once from the bedside, where the doctor and another man sat.

"Thank God you're home!" she said softly. Her eyes were troubled. "When the storm came up, I was worried. Did you find anything?"

"Rain washed out any tracks. Soon as I can I'll search for Red north of here. Maybe he was seen somewhere."

She nodded tiredly. "Jess, there's another problem."

"Mr. Whitley?" he asked quickly, glancing toward the bed.

"He's conscious, and feeling better, I think. But the doctor is concerned about him. Mr. Guthrie came in awhile ago with worrisome news."

"Guthrie?"

"Joe Ed's lawyer. He prepared—the will." The words seemed difficult for her to say, as if they brought closer the reality of Mr. Whitley's dangerous condition. She drew a deep breath and continued. "Someone stole a copy of Joe Ed's will from Mr. Guthrie's office last night. He came out here as soon as possible."

"Is Joe Ed worried about it?"

There was pride in the glance she turned toward the man in the bed. "He took it calmly. He had to be told, even though his own copy of the will is here, and Mr. Guthrie has already written out a new copy and had Joe Ed sign it. Joe Ed was far more distressed to learn that you'd ridden out. Something seems to be preying on his mind where you're concerned. I've never seen him take to anyone the way he has to you."

Jess was embarrassed. "He and my pa were friends."

"It's more than that." She touched his arm. "Mr. Guthrie seems to be finished. Please go and speak to Joe Ed so he'll stop fretting."

McClaren moved forward, conscious of a curious look from the lawyer.

He leaned over the rancher, saddened by the change in him. The mark of impending death was on Joe Ed. Jess had seen it in his own father's face, and he knew instinctively that the days of the man before him were numbered. He felt a deep sense of regret.

"How are you, sir?" he asked.

"Better, son." His voice was weak and hoarse. "You—find Red?"

"No sir. But I will find him, I promise you."

Whitley shook his head. His mouth showed the indomitable will that had carved this ranch out of wilderness, fought drought and freeze and cow thieves. "If they was—lookin' to git him—it's too late already. They'll pick you off too. I need you—" He gasped for breath and the doctor gave Jess a warning look. "Need you here to watch after Maggie and the—the boy."

"Whatever you say, sir," Jess reassured him. "Now you'd best get some sleep, or these gentlemen will throw me off the place."

Whitley tried a smile and grasped Jess's hand as strongly as he was able. He seemed to be trying to convey something with his eyes, pleading for something. His eyes moved to Maggie, and back to Jess.

Jess knew what the old man was asking. How could

he refuse him now? He'd be lying if he tried, and his pride be damned! He loved Maggie. If she would have him, he'd gladly spend his life giving her the happiness she deserved. He squeezed Joe Ed's hand. "You're still boss here, sir," he said meaningfully. "I take your orders. All your orders."

The relief on Whitley's face was good to see. His grip loosened. Jess stepped away, and the doctor leaned over his patient.

Jess left the room, feeling a mixture of satisfaction and trepidation. All very well for him to magnanimously agree to marry Maggie Bourne—but what if she had different ideas? She seemed to care for him, but Jess McClaren wasn't a man to count unhatched chickens. Maggie Bourne had a mind of her own.

Chapter Fifteen

Morning dawned hot and bright, the canyon fragrant and rain-washed. Jess worked near the house, edgy with the need to search for Red Warner, held by his worry about Joe Ed Whitley's illness.

He split piñon and oak wood for the cookstove. Wielding the ax helped his restlessness. Yet he continually watched the trail from the ridges, hoping to see Warner riding in.

Where could Red have gone, the night he left so secretively? Where was he now? Lying dead in some gully, brought down by the men who harassed J-bar-W?

Joey stayed with Jess until after noon, when the dullness of wood splitting apparently palled on him.

"I want to saddle my pony and practice roping calves," he complained.

"Ask Maggie," McClaren said.

Joey frowned but obeyed. Jess was certain Maggie

would refuse permission, but Joey was in the house only moments before he reappeared and raced toward the corrals.

"Don't ride far!" Jess called after him. A short time later he saw the boy spurring his long-suffering pony at a lope up the canyon.

He watched Joey out of sight, a trifle uneasy. Maybe they should have kept the boy close by. Yet it was bad for him to be so involved in his grandfather's illness, and to hang around the house with little to do. He'd work off some energy and be more manageable when he came back after running the legs off his patient horse.

When the wood was stacked, Jess went to the house to ask about Joe Ed. Manuela was stirring a pot of beans at the stove. She shook her head sorrowfully. "He is just as he was. Mostly he sleeps." She dabbed at her eyes with a corner of her apron. "I think he is *muy enfermo,* Señor McClaren."

"So do I, Manuela." Jess turned away. "I'll be at the corrals if you need me."

He caught up Capitan, brushed and groomed the big stud, and reset his shoes. It was soothing to spend the quiet afternoon in the company of the horses, with the sound of the rasp against the bay's hooves, the acrid scent of the corral soil, damp from last night's rain, the cooing of a dove in a stand of pine up on the hill.

It was near sunset when Maggie called to him, her voice urgent.

He ran to meet her. "Is he worse?"

"No, no." She stopped to catch her breath. "I can't find Joey. Have you seen him?"

Jess relaxed. "He just rode up the canyon aways to chase the calves. Didn't you tell him it was all right?"

"He didn't ask me. I saw him in the hallway looking in at his grandfather and I—oh Jess." She raised anguished eyes to him. "I spoke sharply to him. I told him to go to his room and look at his picture books. He must have gone right after that. That was hours ago!"

"Easy now. I'll go get him."

"Would you go quickly? I know it's foolish of me, but there have been so many strange things that I—I can't help being worried, somehow."

"No one would want to harm a little boy, Maggie. I'll find him and bring him back."

He sent her back to the house and threw a saddle on the bay.

His thoughts as he started up the trail in the gathering dusk were more of Maggie than of Joey. She was wearing herself out, trying to nurse Whitley with no help at all from Anna.

Abruptly Jess's thoughts shifted as he realized that he had ridden several miles up the canyon, past two small bunches of cows and calves. There was no sign of Joey. He stopped his horse and called to the child. There was no answer.

Automatically he got down to study the trail. After the rain, the pony's tracks would stand out plain if Joey had come this far.

He found the tracks at once. From the length between the marks and the depth they cut into the earth, Jess knew Joey had been traveling at a fast trot.

He drew in his breath sharply. What tracks were these intermingled with Joey's pony's? Big tracks, bigger than any of the J-bar-W mounts. He'd seen those tracks before, somewhere—

McClaren felt a cold shock. He was in the saddle in one smooth leap, touching spurs to Capitan's sides as he jerked out the Winchester. He sent the thoroughbred scrambling at full speed up the winding, rocky trail.

Jess was still riding hard when the darkness fell. He had traced the boy's horse and that of his companion two miles or so south along the crest trail. There the tracks turned down a canyon into a tangled, untraveled break in the ridge leading east. There the trail vanished, and the darkness did not allow further searching. It was damned hard to make himself rein the bay in. He must not override the tracks. With a feeling of failure, Jess turned back.

His thoughts remained behind, at the point where

the trail had disappeared. Someone had taken care to make the tracks disappear.

Grimly Jess made plans. He would need help to search that vast tangle of canyons east of the ridge, skillful riders and provisions for several days' ride. Recklessly he put his horse to a lope that ate the miles.

He found Maggie watching anxiously for him, the lighted doorway outlining her slender form.

"Jess?" she called as she heard his approaching hoofbeats. "Joey? Is that you?"

José came from somewhere. Jess handed him Capitan's reins, and the boy took the stud back to the corrals.

"I didn't find him, Maggie," he said.

She stared at him, her hands twisting together. He saw her throat move as she swallowed. "You can't find him? I don't—"

"Honey, listen." He gripped her shoulders to steady her. "Quiet now. I'll tell you everything, but I want George Owens and Manuela's boys to hear it, and I *don't* want Mr. Whitley to. Where's Owens and Concepcion?"

"At the bunkhouse, I suppose."

"All right. Come with me."

He led her quickly along the path to the crew's quarters and called Owens, Brissom, and Concepcion outside. They came, Owens hurriedly cramming his hat on his head, Brissom dragging his boot heels, hands in his pants pockets. Damn the shiftless cur, Jess thought savagely. Curly was showing all his usual enthusiasm for a job.

"José?" he called.

"*Aqui, Señor.*" The young man came at a run from the corrals.

"Men," Jess said. "We've got trouble."

Beside him, Maggie drew in her breath sharply. "Jess, tell me what's happened to my boy!" Her face was white in the light from the doorway. Owens watched the two of them intently.

Jess squeezed Maggie's hand. "Someone came into the upper canyon this afternoon and took Joey."

Maggie gasped, and her fingers jerked convulsively

in his. "What do you mean, somebody took him?" she cried.

"Joey was on his old pony, chasing calves a couple, three miles up toward the crest. Someone riding a big horse was there too. Joey's pony's tracks left the canyon right behind another rider. I think that rider forced the boy to go along."

Maggie's face turned toward the blackness of the ridges, the movement as jerky as if performed by a wooden doll. "Daniel," she whispered.

"We don't know that, Maggie," lied McClaren. He couldn't tell her that he *had* known, since the moment he'd recognized the outsized horse tracks, the same ones he'd studied the day Cal Pardue prevented him from following them. He felt now a sick, helpless fury, a compulsion to take instant action.

Maggie jerked her fingers away. "Don't try to humor me! It's Daniel. He's stolen my son away!"

Her voice rose, quavering. She pressed both hands over her mouth as if to keep in screams.

"You may be right, Maggie." Jess tried to reassure her. "But he wouldn't harm the boy. After all—"

"After all, he's the boy's father!" she finished for him. "Do you think that means anything to Daniel?"

"No man would hurt his own boy, a boy he's seeing for the first time. It's a—it's a proud thing to have a son," Jess said, fumbling for words.

She shook her head frantically. "You don't know Danny Whitley," she said. "You don't know him! He's capable of anything. We have to get my boy out of his hands. Jess, please! We have to get Joey away from that evil man!"

She sobbed harshly, her control crumbling. She trembled like an aspen in a windstorm. He put his arm around her, held her close.

"We will, Maggie. We won't rest until we've found Joey. We can't stay on the trail in the dark, but we can ride to the place where I lost the tracks, wait there until first light."

"Yes. Yes, go quickly, please!"

Jess straightened. "Brissom, rope out a fresh horse for me, and a packhorse. José, you and Concepcion saddle up as fast as you can. You'll go with me. Curly, you ride to Circle P—"

"Tonight?" Curly's lashless eyelids lifted incredulously.

Jess turned on him, his narrowed gray eyes menacing. "Yes sir, tonight! And I mean as fast as you can make it, damn you, or I'll kick your yellow-bellied carcass all the way to Tularosa! Ask Mr. Pardue to put his riders to the search tomorrow. I'll draw you a map of where we'll be starting from. When you've given Mr. Pardue my message, you borrow a fresh horse, get to Clear Rivers spread, and ask them for help too. Owens, you stay here with Maggie. Stall Mr. Whitley if he asks questions. He can't be told about the boy. Keep his mind easy."

"Son, I wish to God I was a-ridin' with you," the older man muttered.

"I need you here."

"Jess, you'll need food and bedrolls." Maggie was in control of herself again. "I'll find what you need."

Within an hour the men were on their way. José and Concepcion talked together in soft liquid Spanish as they rode, the words taking on a grieving sound. Both were fond of the little boy. Jess remained silent, alert for any sound, any hint the country they passed through might give him. But there was nothing, only wind-disturbed quiet.

They made a cold camp, with a supper of jerky and cold biscuits. Coffee would have been good in the chill of the mountain night, but a fire would advertise their presence here.

Jess wished desperately for dawn. He thought of Joey, of the child's trusting eyes, his mischief and endless questions, and he vowed inwardly that if Daniel Whitley so much as bruised Maggie's son, he'd pay hard and heavy for it.

Instinctively he felt that Maggie was right that only Daniel could have Joey, just as Jess was certain it had to be Daniel who'd stolen Whitley's will from the lawyer's office. He'd wanted to know how he stood as to inheriting the ranch. When he got the word that Joe

Ed was sick, maybe dying, he had slipped into the ranch house to get a firsthand look at his father. What he now meant to do with Joey was more than Jess could figure. It had to be tied in, somehow. And if Maggie was right about Daniel having no feeling even for his own son, then Joey might well be in danger.

Bitterly McClaren blamed himself for not watching the child more closely. It simply had not occurred to him that Whitley would make his move through his little son. But who could understand the thinking of a man like Daniel?

Daylight was a faint glow in the east when Jess rolled out of his blankets, built a tiny fire for coffee, and got the boys up. They made a quick breakfast while Jess readied the horses. He hobbled the packhorse and left him near water and grass, and stashed most of the supplies to be picked up later.

As soon as it was possible to see, they went to work to find the direction Joey's abductor had taken. The tracks had been removed, but there were still signs to be discovered by the knowledgeable eye: a broken weed, a freshly scratched rock, a hair from a horse's tail caught in oak brush. Slowly they deciphered those signs into a consistent direction. Soon the men discovered tracks once more, leading north and a bit east.

They made fair time until the trail ran into the spreading swath of a rockslide. The three riders split up and began to search for tracks leading out of the ribbon of broken stone where the tumbled rock had spilled down the steep slope at some long-forgotten time, searching for signs that would reveal where the two horses had left it. It was infuriatingly slow work, as the three men slid and climbed along the rocks for a half mile before Concepcion signaled the finding of sign. They redoubled their efforts. Jess felt fierce joy when he found a partial hoofprint leading off the stones and into the brush.

He called the others to the spot. They began to work their way through the nearly impenetrable oak thicket along the shoulder of the mountain. For an hour they struggled through the maze of tangled small limbs and twigs that interlaced at a hundred points about the riders. One of the horses grew frantic as the brush clung and pulled at saddles and bedrolls. José controlled him with difficulty, and they continued, branches whipping and scratching at men and horses until all bore bloody marks.

The tracks led at last into a faint game trail, and the men were able to make better time.

When they emerged from the brush, they were near the crest far north of the trail to J-bar-W. Whoever had taken Joey had doubled craftily back. Only the most tedious tracking could have traced the two horses this far. Jess was grimly aware of the hours it had taken. Hours that may well have been vital to Joey.

The trail now lay roughly parallel to the main crest trail taken by most riders, but it was several hundred yards under the ridge and well concealed. Concepcion remarked that he had not known of this trail, though he often hunted near here.

It was possible to travel at a good pace here. Jess's hopes rose as they spurred their mounts along the twisting, rocky path, careful never to lose sight of those distinctive tracks pressed into earth still damp from the recent cloudburst.

For hours they rode, pausing to rest the horses where the tracks abruptly left the trail for a narrow ridge, eastward.

Jess let out a low exclamation as he suddenly realized that under the tracks he so painstakingly followed lay the nearly obliterated, older tracks of numerous cattle. Only a few tracks had survived the rain, but there was ample sign that cattle had been driven this direction.

"The cow thieves, Mr. McClaren?" Concepcion asked softly.

Jess nodded grimly. "We'd better hide our horses and fan out. Be as quiet as you can, and keep your guns ready."

They led the three horses into concealment some distance off the ridge, and the three moved softly forward on foot.

They hadn't far to go. Abruptly the tracks led off the ridge at an angle. At a gesture the two Mexican boys crept along the ridge to either side of Jess, vanishing in the undergrowth. Both boys were fine hunters, and could move through the brush as silently as deer. Jess wondered if they could be hunters of men if the test should be put to them, as it well might be, at any moment.

Quietly Jess faded through the trees, down the steep, thickly wooded mountainside, until he found a place that offered a view into the narrow canyon.

What he saw made him draw a slow breath. The canyon widened into a bowl that would be invisible from the crest trail, much traveled and only a mile to the west, or from commonly used canyon trails to north and south. Below the grassy, open bowl there appeared to be only a very cramped, narrow exit toward the mouth of the canyon, miles eastward. A meager thread of stream ran by the tortuous trail that would lead out of this little-known fold in the mountains.

And there were cattle. Jess estimated some ninety head visible from his vantage point alone. They grazed contentedly in the high bunch grass of the bowl. And they carried the J-bar-W earmark.

But the cattle were unimportant now. Somewhere down there a man bent on some vicious scheme had taken Maggie's son.

Forcing down impatience, Jess studied the canyon with care. He could see no riders, no camp. Carefully he eased downward again, guarding every step lest a dislodged stone or crackle of broken brush alert unseen watchers below. He forced himself to move unhurriedly. Joey's captor must not be alerted, or there would be no chance at all to get to the boy.

Jess paused often to search the landscape for a campfire, a corral, any sign that the man he sought was present.

At last he spotted a shelter, little more than a lean-to made of poles and brush, almost completely hidden under an overhanging rock ledge. A dying campfire sent up a bare breath of smoke, and a horse stood patiently in a makeshift corral. Jess's throat tightened when he recognized Joey's pony. It moved about the pen, limping badly on the right foreleg.

After a moment two other horses came into view, hobbled and grazing near the stream. Neither was more than average in size. Where was the horse Joey's abductor had ridden? From the depth and size of the track, Jess knew it should be at least sixteen hands, and much heavier than these mustangs.

He watched, anxiety ticking explosively within him, but he saw no more horses, nor any human form.

Again he began his descent. A tiny movement to his left showed him where Concepcion was also moving down, quiet as the wisp of smoke from the campfire.

It took many minutes to complete the downward climb. Once in the valley floor Jess crept nearer the pole shelter. A sound froze him in his tracks. Someone in the lean-to was moaning, a steady, chilling sound.

Jess abandoned caution and ran forward. If the boy had been harmed—

But it was not Joey who lay inside. It was Red Warner. What had been done to him made Jess gag.

The job would have done credit to a vengeful Apache. Someone had carved up Warner's face and hands. There were bullet wounds in his chest and belly. He was dying, but the dying was slow and hideous.

Jess knelt near the cowboy. "Red, can you hear me? It's McClaren. Who did this to you?"

He had to repeat his question before Warner seemed to become aware of him.

"Water!" Red gasped through raw lips. Jess signaled to José, who hurried toward the stream with a tin cup that had been left at the coals of the fire. Concepcion was standing watch against surprise.

"Red," Jess said urgently. "Where's Joey? Tell me who did this?"

It took a long time to get the story. Warner was in bad shape, hanging on to life by a thread.

"I—come to warn him you was—onto him." His face, what was left of it, contorted with indescribable agony.

"You came to warn Daniel? You knew he was behind the thieving!"

The wounded man's eyes held Jess with pitiful entreaty. "Didn't know—what he—is. Knew him all his life. Never thought—what happened could be—all his fault." He moaned. "An'—there was Anna."

"You love Anna, so you helped Daniel," Jess muttered. "Even against Joe Ed." In spite of Red's suffering, Jess felt himself draw away inwardly from the man who had betrayed an old man who trusted him. "You helped Daniel run off stock. Did you tell him where his daddy would be riding the day Daniel took a shot at him?" he asked bitterly. "And what about the two who jumped us—did you lead them to me?"

"No!" Red made a useless effort to rise. "No, McClaren. Anna's—brother—in Roswell. She knew Joe Ed sent for you, she wrote her brother—"

"And he set those two on my trail." Jess nodded. "But you saved my life! Why, Red, if you were working with Anna and Daniel?"

"Didn't know she'd wrote—her brother. An' "—incredibly a grim smile flickered—"I just purely—hate a—backshooter."

"What about the attack on Mr. Whitley, from ambush?" Jess demanded. "And Quilter—you said he was your friend!"

Warner's ghastly face moved from side to side. "I faced Danny with that. He—said it wasn't him. Said it must've been somebody else with—with a grudge. He was only—gonna take his share of what shoulda been—his by rights—"

"And you were fool enough to believe him?"

Warner moaned, blood bubbling from his lips. Jess stared at him, sickened. "Why did your buddy do this to you?"

Warner turned his head wearily. Jess saw he was weakening fast. "He—ordered me to bring Joey to him, to get—Maggie to marry him," the dying man gasped.

"*You* took Joey?"

Warner's nostrils flared, and his voice was momentarily stronger. "God, no! Wouldn't—do—that!"

"So he cut you up?" Jess held Warner's shoulders, held the water to his lips.

Red swallowed painfully and struggled to speak. “Him—and his men.”

“How many riding with him? Where’s he gone?” Jess demanded as the cowpuncher’s eyes flickered shut. “Warner! You got to tell me!”

Red opened his eyes, but they weren’t focusing. “Two. That feller who followed us to steal your horse. He’s with—and—one other—”

“Where! Where, Red?”

But it was too late. Mumbling a word Jess couldn’t catch, Red made a final, convulsive movement, his breath rattled out harshly, and he was gone.

Concepcion touched Jess’s shoulder. “I will find which way they rode out.” His eyes burned. Listening to Red had transformed the quiet, peace-loving young man into a dangerous one.

“We dig a grave, *señor*?” José asked.

“No time now,” Jess said. “The boy’s got to be found. Spread out, look for the tracks.”

Ten minutes later they found them, heading west, toward the crest trail.

Jess tasted bile. “They’re headed back toward the ranch. He knows he’s drawn most of the men away. And he’s an hour or more ahead of us.”

“We must get the horses!”

“You boys get them. I’ll take one of the mounts they left and light out now.”

Concepcion was already running to catch one of the hobbled horses. Jess made a hackamore from a discarded piece of rope hanging on the corral.

He leaped upon the animal bareback and dug in his spurs. The horse was a good one, a sorrel gelding with legs set well under, short-bodied and powerful, but with good reach. He sprang forward and tried to get his head down to buck. Jess kept a firm grip on him and spurred him into a run. Even as José and Concepcion started for the place where they’d hidden the horses, Jess was racing up the slope toward the rim of the canyon.

Chapter Sixteen

Daniel and his men had a frightening start. Jess was thinking furiously as he let the sorrel catch his wind at the crest, struggling to find any gleam of hope in the situation. Perhaps there was one. A small one. Daniel Whitley couldn't be expecting pursuit this soon. He had covered the entrance into the hidden canyon devilishly well. He and the boy had spent the night at the shack, with Red Warner and the other two men, had lingered for breakfast before moving out as the warm ashes of their fire proved. He must have felt very secure.

McClaren gazed unseeingly out over the canyons on the west side of the range and the immensities of wild, broken land beyond. He wasn't enjoying the magnificent view. It was Maggie's image that filled his grim thoughts.

Red had said Daniel meant to force Maggie to marriage. The reason was obvious. He knew about Joe Ed's will, leaving the J-bar-W to Maggie. Marriage would give Daniel what the will denied him.

Urgency gripped McClaren. If it was humanly possible, he must reach the ranch ahead of Whitley's bunch—before Daniel reached Maggie.

Jess gathered the sorrel with a touch of rein and spur, and let the lively little horse run along the crest trail. Daniel's bunch would not have taken this open, well-traveled route. But it was the most direct, and offered the best footing for a running horse. Jess set himself and the cowpony to a pace calculated to get the most speed without exhausting the horse too soon.

He met two groups of riders, searchers from Clear River and Circle P. Jess halted only long enough to say the stolen cattle had been found, but not the boy. He asked the other horsemen to fan out and try to trail Whitley, in case he had not taken the boy to J-bar-W as Jess believed.

He rode on, relieved that others would be covering the possibility that he had guessed wrong. If the kidnappers had headed for the border, these determined riders would discover it.

Reining in at the head of Venado, Jess searched the trail. There were no tracks resembling the ones he'd searched out since dawn. His heart sank. Was he making a mistake, coming straight to the ranch?

Yet there were other, less open trails down to the ranch house. Very likely Daniel would have taken one of those.

Jess urged his tired horse down the trail. He traveled at a trot now, eyes everywhere at once. Daniel might have placed a lookout.

McClaren met no one. Apparently Daniel Whitley was supremely confident, fearing nothing that his father or the J-bar-W hands might do.

A cold sense of purpose settled over Jess. He checked the loads of his Colt and rifle.

Half a mile from the headquarters, Jess released his horse and worked his way along the hillside north of the house.

He found a place that offered a view of the ranch buildings and paused to study the scene below.

In the backyard there were horses, one of them his own bay stud. Two men were mounted, armed with rifles. A big man stood between the horsemen and the porch. Jess could see Joey, held hard against the larger figure. He could also see the handgun Daniel Whitley held against the boy's tousled head. An anger greater than anything Jess had ever experienced roared in his skull at the sight of Joey's helpless position.

Maggie stood on the lowest porch step, her rigid stance expressive of iron control. God, what she must be suffering, seeing her little son in the grasp of the man she hated and feared!

Grimly, Jess worked his way down the slope.

It took a long minute to reach the bunkhouse. He

searched for a way to get into a better position. If only he could get a clear shot at Daniel.

From boyhood he'd held in contempt any man who shot from ambush. Yet now, with Joey's safety at stake, he'd have thrown away his scruples and taken whatever shot was offered. But there was no chance of it. One of the riders with Daniel, the Mexican who had escaped from Jess in Las Cruces, sat his rat-tailed paint squarely between McClaren and Daniel. The dark little man was nervous, alert for any movement or sound, his rifle held ominously ready.

The other outlaw was slightly more relaxed. From his useless vantage point Jess could see the man's wide grin. Evidently he was enjoying the argument between Daniel and Maggie.

"For God's sake, let him go, Daniel!" Maggie's voice reached Jess. "Please. I—I beg you. Let Joey go!"

Daniel laughed. "Sure honey. Just as soon as you come out here and get on this nice horse we saddled for you. Ain't it lucky I found this dandy bay stud handy there in the corral? I get you, and a mighty fine horse!"

"I won't go with you!" Maggie flared, but Jess could see the anguish of indecision in her face. Her hands were clenched as she stepped further out in the yard, as if drawn irresistibly to her son.

"I do believe you got 'er on your line, Whitley." The bearded outlaw laughed, spitting a stream of tobacco juice.

McClaren fingered his Winchester. He could take the two gunmen before Whitley knew what was happening. But if any of the men pulled a trigger, Maggie was in the way, and Joey was a shield for Daniel. McClaren's jaw clenched. His mind searched for the right move to make.

"Go get your prettiest dress, Maggie honey. You and me are gonna do it up right, this time. You gonna be Miz Daniel Whitley by nightfall, just like you always wanted. Seems like you ought to show a little gratitude, since you got this here bastard, and him needin' a name!"

He must have hurt Joey. The boy yelled, a mixture of pain and fury. "Quit it!" he screeched. "Maggie, make him let me go!"

Manuela, hovering in the kitchen door, must have been driven past caution. She made a sudden dart down the steps and toward the three men. There was one shot. Manuela went down with a gurgling scream. Maggie cried out and fell to her knees beside her friend.

"You cowardly brute!" she raged at Daniel. Frantically she tried to lift the other woman, who lay moaning. Maggie was weeping now. It was evident that she was as helpless as a fish in a net.

"Now then, I'm through playin'," Daniel said coldly. "Get up from there, and climb on this horse!"

Desperate, Jess ducked back, circled the bunkhouse, and took the chance of creeping alongside Maggie's garden fence to get in line with Whitley. If any one of the outlaws had happened to glance his way, he could not have failed to see Jess. But their attention was held by Joey, who let out another enraged squall and rained kicks on Whitley's shins, twisting frantically in his father's grip.

"Ow!" yelled Whitley as Jess made it to a big, low-spreading juniper tree and flattened himself to the ground, rifle raised to his cheek.

"You damned brat—why the little hellion has bit me!" Daniel let out a string of oaths.

Jess saw Joey jerk himself almost loose, held only by one shirtsleeve. Then Daniel swept viciously down with his gun barrel, and there was a sickening thump as it struck the side of the child's head. Joey fell, lay crumpled and still on the hard-packed earth.

Maggie's scream as she flung herself toward her boy was covered by the roar of gunfire.

Jess saw his own first shot connect with the bearded gunman's head. The man tumbled from his saddle like a kid's ragdoll. Jess fired again, at the Mexican, burned his left shoulder. He levered another shell into the .30. Someone else had opened fire. Another rifle was in action. Jess had Daniel in his sights. He fired, missed.

Jess rolled out of the juniper's shelter as bullets

stitched the soil near him. He came up, crouching, trying for another clear shot at Daniel. But the big man, one shoulder bloody, slapped Maggie away from Joey and quickly scooped up his unconscious little son. Almost in the same movement, he was into the saddle of his big black and spurring off down the trail.

Jess sprinted for Maggie. The Mexican, trying to control his plunging horse, had dropped his rifle, but his pistol was leveled at Jess. But the shot that boomed was not his. Jess glanced at the kitchen door, amazed to see Joe Ed, face white as death. The old man was held up by George Owens, but the sick man's eyes blazed fire, and he held his Henry rifle steady. But it wasn't needed again. The Mexican was dead, shot through the heart.

Jess reached Maggie, lifted her shoulders. There was a mark on her temple and a thin line of blood trickled down her face. She struggled to her feet.

"Jess, saddle a horse for me—your mare! She'll be faster than any of ours. We must go after Daniel. Joey's hurt—"

"I'll go. Wait here."

Her eyes would have daunted a grizzly. "I'm going with you. I'll be ready in a moment."

There was no time to argue. Jess leaped onto Capitan and raced for the stables. As he transferred Maggie's saddle from the bay to the black mare, Concepcion and José spurred down the trail to the corrals. Quickly Jess told them what had happened.

"Your mother is hurt, boys. You must tend to her. Maggie's riding with me to catch up with Daniel and Joey." He took his own saddle and blanket from the horse José led, and flung them onto Capitan's sleek back, mounted swiftly.

He took the mare's reins, led her behind Capitan at a lope to the house. Maggie was bandaging Manuela. She signaled Jess and José to carry the injured woman into the house. Maggie disappeared into her room, was back in a moment, wearing men's trousers and a shirt, worn boots, and a wide-brimmed hat. She looked like a slim boy, if you didn't notice her wide, anguish-shadowed eyes. She was suffering as only a woman, a mother, could suffer.

Quickly she and McClaren were on their way, bent low over their horses' necks. Maggie's slender body fitted itself to the mare's graceful motion, swaying to the pounding rhythm as the mare and Jess's bay swept side by side down the canyon.

They could not hope to keep up this pace for long, Jess knew, but it would serve to make up a few of the lost minutes. And Maggie needed the violent physical action. Jess understood that the terror of her child's situation, the pent-up anxieties of weeks brought now to an unbelievable, cruel crisis, demanded urgent, direct measures.

And so he let Capitan run, holding him in just enough to match the mare's strides.

Maggie rode with instinctive and experienced skill, her face a mask. Jess wondered if she even saw the ground her mount raced over or the tree branches that reached out over the trail to whip across the riders' faces. Maggie bent to avoid the limbs. Yet Jess suspected that it was unconsciously done.

They were pushing the horses too hard. Jess was about to catch the mare's rein and slow the pace. At that moment Maggie drew the black in, the excited mare rearing in protest. Maggie controlled her, reining her in a spin to settle her down.

They stopped to let the horses rest for a few moments. Jess was relieved to see that Maggie's look was more normal. Her eyes were still agonized, but they seemed aware and reasoning.

"Maggie, we'll find him," Jess said quietly.

Wordlessly she reached a hand to him. He caught it. "I'll have to track Daniel's horse," he said. "It will slow us down some."

"I think I know where he's going. He'll head for the Sands."

Jess studied her face. "What makes you think that's where he'll go?"

"I don't think. I know. Daniel's always been fascinated by the White Sands. Most folks avoid the Sands, but he used to go in there often. Sometimes he camped for weeks. I rode with him once or twice when we were just kids. He used to claim that a man could hide in the Sands forever, if he knew the water holes."

"Was there a particular place he liked to go?"

She shook her head. "He just used to ride, I think, and camp wherever he happened to be—probably never far from water, but I don't know—"

Urgently, Jess interrupted. "Was there a particular trail he used?"

Miserably, she shook her head.

"Then we'll have to keep those tracks in sight. I promise you we'll move as fast as possible."

With that, he nudged the stud and the horses moved at a trot along the canyon trail and out onto the desert. Jess paused now and then to be sure they were still on the tracks of Daniel's Morgan gelding.

It wasn't difficult. Daniel had made no apparent effort to conceal the tracks. He, like Maggie and Jess, had slowed his pace to one a horse could endure for long hours. The trail led southwest across the basin, ignoring the turnoff toward Tularosa. It appeared that Maggie was right. Daniel was heading for the White Sands.

Chapter Seventeen

They rode steadily, silently. The sun was setting as they moved into the edges of the Sands, gradually leaving behind the red desert soil and the thicker vegetation.

The edge of the sands was nearly overgrown with brush. Growth gradually became less and less as the riders moved further into the pale wasteland, until there was virtually nothing to be seen but sand.

Looking out over the weird landscape, Jess felt an

uneasy stirring of his instincts. The smooth, cream-white dunes, great swells of fine, wind-sculptured gypsum, rose and fell about them. When they were at the crest of a sand ridge, they could see the distant blue line of the San Andreas. The Sands gave an impression of complete desolation, utter lifelessness. The impression was false. Snakes, mice, lizards had somehow learned to survive here.

But this strange stretch of earth held no welcome for man. Very few travelers ventured far into the eerie white desert that could alter its landmarks within the space of hours. Even established trails must yield to the fierce urging of the winds that could very rapidly shift dunes consisting of many tons of sand. Where the sand mountains themselves must be crossed, it taxed horses to find footing in the deep, unstable stuff. Often the riders must dismount and lead their struggling horses diagonally up the steep slopes.

So far, the tracks of Daniel's horse remained clear, so plainly marked that at every dune crest it seemed the pursuers might hope to catch a glimpse of Whitley and the child. But the tracks led tantalizingly further and further into the Sands, with never the briefest glimpse of the horse and riders that had left those tracks.

"If the wind rises"—Maggie spoke the fear that they both felt—"it could wipe out the trail in five minutes. Can't we hurry, Jess?"

"We're tiring these horses too much as it is," he called back to her. "We may need them bad, later."

Anguished, she nodded. They plodded on.

Fortunately, the evening remained windless, but there was another factor working against them. The summer night was slow in falling, but it must grow dark at last. Jess spurred Capitan on until he could no longer make out the tracks.

He halted the stallion. Maggie reined in alongside.

"Jess?" she whispered. He had never heard such uncertainty in anyone's voice.

"No use pushing on. Too much chance of losing the trail entirely. There'll be a moon later. We'll wait and rest the horses."

He expected her to argue, to plead for continuing. She said nothing. He imagined the cost of her compliance. Her silence was somehow more eloquent than a cry of sheer desperation.

Jess loosened the cinches, wishing he had had time to bring grain for the horses, wishing there was water for them. He went to Maggie and took her rigid body into his arms.

"We'll find him, Maggie. You have my word."

Abruptly her control broke. She cried wildly, and he held her until she was still.

"I'm sorry, Jess," she murmured against his shirt.

"Sit down and try to rest," he said. "I'm going to climb to the top of the next dune and see if there's any sign of a campfire."

He felt the sudden surge of her hope. "Yes! Oh Jess, maybe they aren't far ahead!"

"Maybe." But he felt certain Daniel Whitley would not be fool enough to guide them to his camp. He left her and climbed the highest nearby dune.

A light breeze played with the sand crystals, fanning them for a moment into the air like a wispy veil. The night was cooler than the brutal day, yet still uncomfortably warm. Even the sand was warm to the touch as Jess knelt on one knee to survey the surrounding country.

As he had feared, there was no flicker of campfire. There was no sound save the breeze and a hiss of sand as it slid over the sharp face of the dune, dislodged by Jess's movement.

All that could be seen was the pale expanse of sand, reaching out on all sides, broken in the far distance by the darker line of the mountains. It was too dark now to make out any detail. Only the vague contours of dunes could be distinguished.

Jess went back to Maggie and the horses. He had hoped she might sleep while she had the opportunity, but she sat as he had left her, hugging her knees, staring into the darkness. Her hair had come down around her shoulders, a rich, dark fall that framed her slim, pale face. Her eyes were hidden in shadow. Jess wished he had the power to comfort and relieve her fears. All he could do was share them.

At the first lifting light of the moon, Jess led the mare to Maggie and gave her the reins. Lightly she mounted. Jess led out on the trail again, bent low to be sure of the prints in the sand.

Throughout the night, until the moonlight once more deserted them, they followed a trail that might have been made by a phantom, for all the gain they seemed to make.

Apparently Whitley was not merely aiming to cross the Sands. It was as if he played a game with them, leading them without any particular goal in mind among the endless dunes. Sometimes the path doubled back sharply for as much as a mile. McClaren could only grit his teeth with anger and frustration, knowing that fifteen minutes or an hour before, Daniel might have passed only a few hundred yards to one side of them, hidden by the rolling sand hills. Or perhaps he had watched them, laughing to himself as they plodded along his trail.

"He's playing with us!" Maggie cried out once. "Jess, all this riding is terrible for Joey. He's hurt, who knows how badly? He must be worn out."

"Don't fret, Maggie," Jess tried to reassure her. "The boy's probably asleep."

Or dead.

He might as well have spoken the grim thought. It shouted itself into the night. Even in the ghostly dim moon-and-sand radiance, he saw Maggie's throat move convulsively.

"All we can do is keep tracking him. He'll have to rest his horse sometime," Jess said.

"Can't we move faster?"

To make her feel better, he urged the stallion to a lope along the single line of hoofprints for the next quarter of a mile, then let him drop back to a trot. The horses would soon be suffering for lack of water and rest and feed. There was no way of knowing when or where such necessities could be found. The horses must be saved as much as possible.

Near dawn, it happened. They rounded a great dune, heading north, eyes gritty with need of sleep, horses stumbling with weariness in spite of a brief rest enforced by the predawn darkness. Maggie saw it first, and let out a strangled cry.

Jess jerked erect in the saddle, taking his eyes from the never-ending file of dish-shaped depressions they had followed for so many long hours. Fifty yards ahead, a blanket-wrapped bundle lay on the ground by the trail. One small boot protruded from it.

"Joey!" Maggie's scream shattered the stillness of the dunes. She spurred the black mare and passed Jess at a run. She was out of the saddle, stumbling and running, before Jess could reach her. Every sense was alert now. Jess smelled a trap.

"Maggie, wait!"

Capitan flung up his head and nickered shrilly. Jess leaped from his horse and caught the woman two steps away from the still bundle. "Maggie, no!"

"Let me go!" she gasped, struggling in his hands.

"Be a gent, McClaren," drawled a cold voice. "Let the lady go."

Jess whirled. At the curve of the dune, Daniel Whitley lay prone, a rifle leveled at them.

"No!" Whitley warned. "Keep your hands away from your gun."

Jess froze, expecting the slam of a rifle bullet in his chest.

Maggie ignored Daniel and flung herself beside the blanketed figure. She touched the blanket, tugged it loose, and went as rigid as stone, hands still outstretched. The little scuffed boot rolled free and lay empty on its side. Sand, molded to the size and shape of a child's body, spilled from the blanket.

Daniel Whitley roared with laughter. "What's the matter, honey?"

Slowly she stood. "Where is he? Where's Joey?"

"Anxious about your boy, are you? Oh, excuse me, *our* boy." He chuckled. "Don't be embarrassed about it in front of McClaren here. He ain't so young that he thinks you found the brat in a cabbage patch. No sir. He won't be surprised to hear that you and I spent a real interestin' night that time. I've never forgot it, Maggie. In fact I can hardly wait to see if you're still as sweet and willing now—"

"Shut your filthy mouth, Whitley," Jess said, his hands aching to choke the power of speech out of Daniel.

"Now would you listen to that?" Daniel Whitley said with exaggerated admiration. "You act like you got the drop on me, McClaren, and here you are counting away your last seconds before you meet your maker."

"Daniel, please!" Maggie cried.

"What is it now, honey? You don't want me to plug Mr. McClaren? Oh, I heard how he's been sweet-talking you, taking you out on the town, just as if you wasn't damaged goods, but a real fine lady!"

"What have you done with Joey?" Jess gritted.

"What business is it of yours?" Whitley sneered. "What do you care about a little ol' woodscolt like Joey? It ain't gonna matter when your mouth is full of sand and the buzzards are helpin' themselves to your hide."

"Please, Daniel, where is he?" Maggie pleaded, face white in the growing dawnlight.

"Come on up here and see. You too, McClaren. Step a little farther away from them horses and that rifle you been edgin' closer to. You come over here and I'll just get a hold on the ponies. Don't want to spook 'em when I shoot. That's a real fancy pair of horses, McClaren. Sure do thank you for delivering 'em, along with my little wife." He stood and moved leisurely toward them, gesturing Maggie and Jess away from the horses.

"I'm not your wife!" the girl spat at him.

He laughed. "Still got spirit, ain't you, sugar? Well, don't pout. You will be my legal spouse real soon. You were so set on it years ago, when all I wanted from you was fun an' games. But now that my lovin' pa, the old fool, has gone and willed everything to you, I reckon I'll have to give in an' do it right. Maybe it won't be so bad. I might get to like breaking you to harness."

Daniel caught up Capitan's reins and then the black mare's, never taking his eyes off his captives. Leading the horses, he herded Jess and Maggie ahead of him over the small dune—and between two towering ones to where his big Morgan gelding stood, head down. With a cry Maggie ran to the figure lying back against the sand. Jess hurried after her. They bent over the boy, Maggie touching the dirty small face anxiously.

"He's alive, Jess," she whispered. "He's breathing, thank God. Joey? Wake up, honey."

The child moved his head and mumbled weakly. Jess turned him gently and examined his head wound. The cut had bled and dried, matting the thick, fair hair. Jess felt the area carefully, with Maggie's tortured eyes on him. There was some swelling, but on the whole the injury seemed not too bad. Only a doctor could say for sure.

Maggie tried to rouse her child, without success.

"Now, if that ain't a pretty little picture," Daniel said.

Jess swung around. Daniel had left Jess's horses near his Morgan. He held his rifle ready, shoving his hat back. Curly black hair lay on his broad forehead. Daniel had a handsome, laughing face. But the man's eyes were cold, pale blue, like wet ice.

Jess felt a chill along his spine. It would be soon now. There could be no advantage to Daniel Whitley in keeping McClaren alive.

"Oblige me by tossing over your handgun, if you please!" Daniel ordered.

The man was crazy, Jess thought. If there was gunfire, the boy and Maggie were too close. Apparently he cared not at all for their safety, not even for Maggie's, in spite of his plan to force her into marriage. But maybe that was not his plan at all, and never had been. Maybe he figured Maggie's death would as surely give him the Whitley property.

It was senseless. Too many people knew now that Daniel was behind the rustling, the attack from ambush on his father, the kidnapping and wounding of his own son. The disappearance of Maggie and Joey would not be overlooked even in this lawless territory.

Pardue and his men, Manuela and her sons, Joe Ed himself would see justice done.

It seemed that Daniel was unable to realize any of this. He would be made to pay, but that was small comfort to the three captives here and now.

"I'm waiting!" snarled Daniel. "Throw out your gun. Now. With your left hand, McClaren.

It was sure death, but it was the only chance McClaren was ever going to get. His mind was cool and steady as he obediently reached to ease the Colt from its holster, twisting his hand to grasp the butt so that there would be no lost motion in bringing the revolver up for shooting. If Daniel noticed the angle of Jess's hand, there would never be time for a shot, or even for lifting the gun from the leather.

There was one tiny factor on Jess's side. As a boy he had practiced shooting with his left hand, with some idea of emulating a much-admired Texas Ranger. Jess had achieved some skill with the left hand. But that was years ago. Would the trick be remembered now by the fingers of his left hand. Would the move be so slow as to be useless?

The die was cast. Willing himself to the act, Jess gripped the gun, brought it around in a blur of movement, and squeezed the trigger.

It was a double explosion of sound as Daniel's rifle boomed a fraction before Jess's Colt. Jess saw Daniel double forward, even as he felt himself lifted and flung backward, and knew he was hit. His gun left his hand, and before he sank into blackness, his mind registered the sound of a third shot.

He came awake to pain and someone pulling at him.

"Jess! You've got to get up. Please Jess."

He was confused. Who disturbed the darkness and peace? He lifted heavy lids. Somebody bent over him, an oval blur of face, a mouth moving, pleading with him, the sound of a voice fading in and out.

He closed his eyes. A hard, stinging slap denied his escape into rest.

"Ahh!" he groaned.

"Jess, listen! You have to get up. Now!"

He blinked, more alert now. Maggie's face was smeared with dirt and blood. She was crying. "Maggie?" he mumbled, and tried to sit up.

Pain ripped aside the last of his stupor, a white-hot stab of agony in shoulder and chest. He gasped.

Maggie supported his shoulders. "You've got to try and stand up," she cried. "I'll help you. You have to get on your horse."

He felt his head whirling again and tried to hold on to consciousness. With effort, he forced the mists away a little.

"Try now, Jess. Be careful. I bandaged your shoulder as well as I could, but you're still bleeding."

Gritting his teeth, vision swimming, he tried to obey her. Halfway to his feet, he remembered what had happened.

"Where's—Daniel?" he croaked. "He's—"

"There," she muttered. "He's over there."

Jess turned his head. There were the horses—or two of them. There in the sand lay Whitley's rifle. With nightmarish slowness McClaren's clouded eyes jerked further and found the enemy.

Daniel Whitley was lying on his side, legs drawn up. Blood from his chest spread in a garish stain, sinking into the white sand. One eye was gone, leaving a red, hideously staring hole. The back of his head was missing.

"I hit him—" Jess mumbled, puzzled. Hadn't he only fired once?

"I grabbed your gun and finished him. I had to," she whispered. "He was going to shoot again."

He felt her shudder, but after a deep breath, she spoke almost naturally. "We have to get out of here. Can you get on the stallion?"

"I'll—get on," he said grimly, hating the tremor of his legs.

"There's no water. The heat will be bad."

Jess saw that Joey was sitting on the ground beside the Morgan. The child was conscious but seemed confused and ill.

After a try or two, Jess managed to get on his horse, then hoped desperately that he could stay on. Maggie lifted Joey to the Morgan's saddle and climbed on behind.

"The mare ran away, Jess. I'm sorry," she said, as if the loss of a horse was of much importance now.

"Never mind," Jess gasped. "Try to get—us home."

But they did not make it to the ranch. They were still a few miles from the edge of the Sands when Jess slid unconscious from his horse. Maggie could not rouse or lift him. She was forced to leave him in the merciless sun and ride on.

Slowly Jess woke to find himself in a bed, in an unfamiliar room. Dr. Potter was replacing instruments in his bag. He turned quickly as Jess made some sound.

"Back among the living, man? About time."

"Doc? What—"

"Now, no long-winded speeches, McClaren. You still got one spur hung in the Pearly Gates. You got a hole in your shoulder that spilled enough blood to kill any normal, self-respecting man. I reckon you didn't have sense enough to give up the ghost. Now then, I know you're worried about Miss Bourne and her boy. I sent Miss Maggie home. Joey's got a concussion. He's in bed at my house. You get some sleep, boy! I'll look in later."

The physician left before Jess could voice any further questions. So it was only later Jess learned that he was a guest in the Tularosa Hotel and would be for some days. After a day and a half, Dr. Potter reluctantly gave him the rest of the news. Maggie would be unable to leave J-bar-W for a time. Joe Ed Whitley was on his deathbed. She was nursing him night and day.

"It was too much for him, seeing what his own son was capable of." Potter shook his head. "Strange how someone like Whitley could sire a damned, vicious fool like Daniel."

"Maggie told you—"

"What happened out on the Sands? Yes. Daniel's body's been brought in. Someone found your mare too—you're right lucky it was an honest man, brought her to town and asked around about her. Cal Pardue and his men rode in to Las Cruces to make a statement to the sheriff. Reckon you'll have to add your two bits when you're on your feet. But nobody's blaming you or Miss Bourne. The story's out how Daniel treated her years ago. Some of the respectable biddies of this town are having to eat crow. Does my heart good, believe me!

"Now then," continued the doctor. "Mrs. Valdez has brought your supper from the café, and she'll help you with it. That's enough talk for one day."

He left, and McClaren had to endure the uncertainty and the loneliness awhile longer.

Three days passed. Joey was up and about, spending a lot of his time with Jess. The boy was quiet and subdued. Once he spoke of his ordeal.

"That—that bad man said he was my pa, Jess. Was he telling a lie?"

"He was your pa, but he didn't deserve to be, son." Jess hoped it was the right thing to tell him. It seemed wrong to lie to the boy.

"He made me go with him, and he hurt me, and he scared Maggie. I hope he never comes around here again."

Jess realized that Joey didn't know what had happened in the Sands. Maybe that was better. There was already far too much for a little boy to have to understand.

"He won't be back, Joey. I promise you that."

"When's Maggie coming to get me?" Joey asked anxiously.

"Soon as she can. You know she wants to be with you."

"With you too, Jess. Maggie likes you," confided the boy. "Jess, is Grandpa sick again? Is that why Maggie don't come and get me?"

Jess hesitated. Sooner or later he'd have to know. Maybe it was best to be straight with him about Joe Ed.

"He's real sick, Joey."

"Is he gonna die?"

"Maybe he will, Joey. He's old. He's about finished all he wanted to do."

Joey nodded and lifted his head in a way that brought Maggie's courage and determination to mind.

"I know, Jess. He told me, and he told me to mind you, just like you was him. But I didn't. You told me to ask Maggie if I could chase the calves, an' I didn't. Maggie made me mad, so I just sneaked off. I'm sorry. I promise I'll mind you like Grandpa told me."

Wordlessly Jess squeezed the child's hand.

Finally the long wait ended. Maggie woke Jess from a restless doze in late afternoon. He couldn't remember ever being so glad to see anyone.

"Maggie!" He held out his hand. She took it between her own and studied him anxiously.

"How do you feel, Jess? Dr. Potter says you can be up by tomorrow."

"I'd better be or I'll grow to this danged bed. How's Joe Ed?"

She bent her head quickly. "He's gone, Jess. This morning, before daylight."

"Oh, damn, honey. I wish I'd been there."

"He spoke of you, only yesterday. I had to tell him what happened to Daniel, what Daniel tried to do. It broke his heart, but he said—in my place he'd have—have done the same. Oh, Jess!"

She buried her face in his shoulder. He held her gently. She sat up and wiped her face. "I'm sorry. I know nothing can be changed now. My shot was the one that killed Daniel. I have to live with that."

"Have you forgotten you saved my life, and maybe your own and the boy's? Have you seen Joey yet?"

She nodded, swallowing. "I told him about his grandfather. He took it hard."

"How's Manuela?"

"She's going to be fine. The bullet went through her side cleanly. She's already up and around a little, thank God."

"She's a fine woman. A good friend." McClaren stirred restlessly. "Maggie, how did Anna take all this? There ain't much to like about that woman, but she's lost her husband and her son. I reckon I pity her."

"I know." Maggie sighed. "I believe Daniel was the only one on earth she ever loved."

"Reckon it was hard for her."

"I don't know. She's been gone from the ranch. She left on horseback the day after Joey disappeared, while you were out searching for him."

"Where did she go?"

"I have no idea. It's the first time in years I can remember Anna getting on a horse. No one seems to know anything about her, but she must have heard about Daniel and Joe Ed by now. She'll be back." She sat quietly for a few moments.

"Jess—" She hesitated oddly.

"What is it?" He saw that her cheek was warmed with color, and she averted her eyes.

"Joe Ed told me—what he asked you to do. That he—wanted you to marry me. And that you refused."

Jess let out a harsh, exasperated breath. "Oh, hell, I wish he hadn't said anything. Let me explain—"

She smiled. "It's all right. Joe Ed told me. About the ranch being willed to me, and how you felt about that. I want to thank you for not taking advantage. It would have been easy. But you never pretended you would be staying."

Her eyes were steady, but there was sadness in their depths.

"Maggie, you don't understand. Don't you know how much I've wanted—don't you know by now there's nothing I'd rather do than to stay here with you. I don't know how I can ride away from you. And—it's wrong to ask you to go with me. I've got nothing, Maggie."

"Neither have I, Jess." Her voice trembled. "Not if you go."

He sat up, ashamed of the effort it required. "Honey," he began helplessly.

"I mean it, Jess."

He groaned and took her in his arms. Nothing had ever felt more right. But that didn't change the circumstances.

"Maggie, you got to see—"

She shook her head fiercely against his chest. "If you go, Joey and I are going with you. When Daniel took Joe Ed's will, Joe Ed had his attorney make a new paper. It gives the J-bar-W to Joey, and names you as Joey's guardian. It gives you the option of buying the ranch, a little at a time, paying the money into a trust fund for Joey, at a fair price Joe Ed set. But if you won't agree, I have the right to do whatever I like with the ranch, in Joey's behalf. I can sell and put the money back for him. Or simply abandon the whole place! Whatever I do, I won't stay there without you."

She was trembling with the intensity of her appeal.

Jess studied her worriedly. "Maggie, you can't mean that. Joe Ed wanted you and Joey to have what he'd worked to build up."

She shook her head stubbornly. "There are more important things."

He argued, but she remained immovable in her determination.

"I see what you're planning, Jess McClaren." She met his eyes steadily. "You'll just ride out without telling me, won't you? Your stubborn pride will keep us from being together!"

It was true that he'd been wondering if he could stand to do just that, and he rubbed a hand over his beard, sheepishly.

"Jess," she said, "if you do that, I'll sell the ranch, much as I love it, much as I want my son to grow up there. Joey and I will follow. We'll find you, if it takes a lifetime."

McClaren took her shoulders in both hands and held her away. "Maggie, what would you have me do?" he asked.

She dropped her eyes, her hands nervously clasped in her lap. "Do you—care for me at all, Jess?"

He let his breath out in surrender. "Oh Maggie, I love you. You know that. I've loved you since the first day I laid eyes on you, holding that damned rifle on me, trying to send me about my business."

Her eyes leaped to his, glowing, joyful, determined.

"Then I want to be your wife. Wherever you go, I want to be with you. Pride means so much to you, but I am throwing mine away."

"If we stay here, there'll be talk. People will wonder—"

"Talk doesn't scare me, Jess McClaren." She gave him a fierce look. "Does it scare you?"

He grinned, feeling suddenly light-headed. "No, ma'am. When can we be married?"

With a cry of delight she was back in his arms. Heart pounding, he kissed her, wondering how he could ever have imagined he could leave her.

At Jess's insistence, Maggie helped him get out of bed, find a shirt, and put on his boots. He felt now that he would be able to tackle anything. A good meal instead of the pap they'd been feeding him, and he'd soon lose the weakness his wound had produced.

"I'm going back to J-bar-W with you and Joey," he announced.

She frowned, touching his arm. "Jess, no. It's too soon. You mustn't ride. The doctor says your wound hasn't fully closed."

But he was not to be deterred. "Go rent a buggy," he ordered. "I can't stay in this blasted room another hour. I'll wait here for you."

Reluctantly she agreed. He sat in a chair by the window, overlooking the street in front of the hotel. The effort of pulling on his boots had left him breathing hard. He watched through the open window as Maggie came out of the building and started for her horse, tied at the hitch rail.

She was almost to the animal when a harsh command from someone out of Jess's sight stopped her. Maggie swung around.

Another figure stepped into view just for an instant, someone dressed in dark trousers and coat, a hat pulled low. He was holding a double-barreled shotgun, and he gestured with it. Maggie moved ahead of the man, into the alley.

Cursing, Jess was on his feet, jerking his Colt from the holster hanging on the bedpost. He slammed open the door and ran, ignoring weakness. He took the stairs two at a time, and was out the front door, his gun in his hand. His head was spinning, breath coming hard.

It was almost dark. Few people were on the street at this time of day. Most folks were home eating supper, resting after the labors of the afternoon. Jess moved close to the hotel wall and crept soundlessly to the corner.

He peered into the alley. There were two figures, halfway along the narrow lane that lay between the hotel and an adobe-walled patio.

Jess eased around the corner, moving slowly and with care toward the small man who held Maggie at gunpoint. Fortunately, the gunman kept his back to the alley entrance. He was saying something—

"You thought you'd won, you little bitch!" hissed Maggie's captor. Jess paused in astonishment. It was not a man threatening Maggie. It was Anna Whitley, her voice rising in hatred and triumph.

"When they said my son was dead, I wouldn't believe it. I knew he had your bastard with him, and I was certain you'd do whatever Danny wanted, to protect your precious brat."

"If you knew he had Joey, you must have helped Daniel plan to kidnap him." Maggie's voice was low, intense with accusation. "Why would you do a thing like that, Anna? You're the boy's grandmother. And why are you skulking around in men's clothing, waving a gun? I know you're grieving—"

"You wanton slut!" Anna spat out, "what do you know about it? Ah, you were the beginning of all our trouble, Joe Ed doting over you like the old fool he was, even turning his son away for you! I vowed I'd make you pay for what you did, and I told my son the best way to make you suffer. I told him to kill the boy! But he thought he had a better idea. He wanted the ranch and the cattle. Joe Ed had left everything to you, the stupid old—"

"Stop it! Joe Ed is dead, Anna!"

Anna seemed startled, but not particularly upset.

"So what if he is? It's long overdue. And so is what I'm going to do to you. You won't be so pretty after this buckshot blasts your face away, you rotten, worthless—"

Desperately, Jess ran, shouting. "Anna, no!"

If he'd expected her to drop her weapon, he was disappointed. She whirled, pulling the trigger, and one barrel blasted, echoing in the narrow alley. If Jess had not flung himself aside, he would have caught the buckshot full in the face. But the slam of his body against the ground brought paralyzing pain that held him for the pivotal moment, a moment that brought Maggie recklessly to his side and allowed Anna to cover them both with the shotgun, one barrel of which was still lethally charged.

"Jess!" cried Maggie. "Oh Jess, are you hit?"

He clenched his jaw, feeling his wound trickling blood, reopened by the fall against the alley's hard-packed ground. His Colt lay many feet away. They stood weaponless against the murderous Anna. At least he would face her on his feet.

"By all means, pick up your lover." Anna tittered shrilly. "I dislike shooting a dog groveling in the dirt."

As Maggie lent him her strength to get to his feet, Jess's hand closed upon half a broken bottle. He concealed it as well as he could in his hand as he braced weak legs apart.

"Maggie," he whispered, "get behind me! Then run!"

"No." She stood erect and proud at his side, one arm still strongly about his waist.

Oh God, Jess thought desperately. Maggie's courage and pride would not let him save her. She would stand right here, pressed close against him, accepting his death as her own.

Jess was aware of people at the end of the alley, drawn, no doubt, by the shotgun blast. But no one had the courage to enter the danger zone.

"You don't want to do this, Mrs. Whitley," Jess said quietly. "There are witnesses. You can't get away."

She laughed, an ugly, mirthless sound. "What does it matter? They won't hang a woman. I'll tell them the little tramp moved into my husband's bed—no one will blame me for doing away with her. As for you,

McClaren, you threatened me with your handgun—what can I do but defend myself?"

They were the words of someone long past sane reasoning. Jess cursed his weakness, spurred his brain savagely for some chance—just a chance to spare Maggie! He found himself praying as he saw Anna lift the shotgun, heard a murmur of astonished excitement from the gathering onlookers at the mouth of the dim alley as they realized that the woman meant to kill Jess and Maggie with no more compunction than a man might step upon a caterpillar.

There was no more time to consider. Jess slammed his outflung left arm back against Maggie's chest pushing her behind him and flat against the building wall. At the same time, he lifted and flung the broken bottle straight into Anna Whitley's face with all the force his injured body and his furiously anguished mind could produce.

The jagged points of the thick glass slashed across her left eye and nose, making a spurting ruin of that carefully preserved white skin.

The impact jerked her head and body back as the shotgun belched in her clenched hands.

Jess was falling back, dragging Maggie with him to the ground, but he had no real hope of escaping death in that shattering moment.

But as Anna screeched at the impact of the broken bottle, the shotgun barrel tilted upward—just enough.

Jess was scrambling to his feet even as the echoes died. and three long strides carried him to Anna Whitley, seated flat on her backside in the garbage-strewn alley, her face streaming blood, wailing like a lost soul. He grabbed the gun.

"Get the doctor!" Jess roared as people struggled for a better look, still afraid to come into the alley. He paused only long enough to roughly assure himself that Mrs. Whitley was carrying no other weapon, then he turned to help Maggie up.

"Dear God, Jess," Maggie whispered. "If you hadn't come—"

"It's all over, honey. She won't try again." Jess held

her close, absorbing the precious warmth of her, feeling her heart pound against his own."

"She's hurt. I must see what I can do—"

But he grasped her shoulders firmly. "Let these people take care of her. You and I are going home."

Maggie took a deep breath and straightened her shoulders. Jess marveled at her strength. Any other woman would have indulged in hysterics. Maggie merely bent to retrieve her hat where it had fallen and set it straight upon her disheveled auburn hair.

Then, smiling wanly, she took Jess's arm and walked with him out of the alley.

About the Author

E. Z. Woods is a rancher in Nogal, New Mexico, not far from the edge of the vast White Sands.